This is the city. Kalamazoo City. Population: 75,000. By day, it's a bright, vibrant metropolis, the kind of city where dreams come true. It is a mecca of business, the arts, sports, and cuisine, and, at the center of it all, is the gleaming facade of Pandini Tower, the jewel of Kalamazoo City. Those who don't live here dream of making it here. And those who do, well, they know that there's just no city like it.

But it is a different city once the sun goes down. The criminal element, asleep by day, haunts certain dark corners at night. Especially the run-down old docks on the south side of town, perhaps the darkest corner of all.

On one particular evening, a rather dapper-looking frog stood looking very much out of place among the riffraff who nightly roamed the docks. He was dressed like a teacher. In fact, he was a teacher. Professor Hopkins.

A lone, flickering streetlamp on the easternmost pier was the only light source. Shadows scattered across the wooden planks like ghosts at the ready to snatch one's soul. Professor Hopkins nervously checked his watch. Three minutes past eleven. The professor was on time, but the guy he was meeting wasn't.

Finally, a whisper came from the shadows. "You come alone, like we said?"

The voice could scarcely be heard, but Professor Hopkins jumped with fright, the dock creaking beneath his feet. "Y-y-yes," he said, composing himself.

"Keep it down!" said the voice. "You should know better by now. You got the money?"

Professor Hopkins nodded and, his hands shaking, pulled an envelope from inside his jacket.

"You're going to drop it right under the streetlamp," said the voice. "I'm going to take the dough and leave you the goods. Any sudden moves, the deal is off, got it?"

"Okay," said the professor, stepping forward and putting the envelope down in the glow of the unsteady streetlight. He heard footsteps, and a furry hand reached out and picked up the envelope.

"Sweet," said the voice. A duffel bag, bursting with something heavy and damp, dropped at Professor Hopkins's feet. "Here's what you asked for. Now, don't you go telling nobody where you got this. Someone asks you, I don't know you, and you don't know me."

And with that, he was gone, the thumping of receding feet soon swallowed by the still night. Professor Hopkins exhaled, took off his jacket, and dropped it

on top of the duffel bag. Perspiration ran down his face. He cleaned his glasses on his dress shirt. Only when he was sure he was alone did he take out his cell phone and begin dialing a number.

"It's me. I have the fish. We need to—"

But before Professor Hopkins could finish his sentence, a car roared out of a nearby warehouse, its headlights blazing a path toward the eastern pier. The professor watched in horror as it picked up speed and barreled toward him. As it bolted past the streetlight, the professor caught a momentary glimpse of the driver.

That would be the last thing Professor Hopkins saw on the pier that night.

Welcome to Kalamazoo City.

Walden Pond Press is an imprint of HarperCollins Publishers.

Platypus Police Squad: The Frog Who Croaked

Library of Congress Cataloging-in-Publication Data is available.
ISBN 978-0-06-207164-4

Typography by Tom Forget
13 14 15 16 17   CG/RRDH   10 9 8 7 6 5 4 3 2 1
❖
First Edition

For my girls—Gina, Zoe, and Lucy

THE ZENGO HOUSE, 6:45 A.M.

Detective Rick Zengo's alarm clock buzzed, but he was already wide-awake. He turned it off, took a deep breath, and sprang up from bed, shoving aside his blankets. Push-ups, sit-ups, tail flexes, jumping jacks. He felt great. No, he felt awesome.

His outfit for the day was carefully draped over his chair—new jeans, a sharp collared shirt, and his lucky leather jacket. He dressed slowly, inspecting himself in the mirror. His tail was looking excellent today. He gave it a wag.

Zengo switched on the radio and tuned in to Z94.3. The bass of hip-hop beats filled Zengo's bedroom as blood pulsated through his veins. He opened the window, letting fresh air stream into his well-organized, enormous, immaculate room. The familiar view from his second-floor bedroom sprawled out before him. Rows of houses with well-maintained yards. Lush greenery adorning the concrete blocks. And beyond that, the skyline of the city he pledged to protect.

It was his turn now.

The temperature was on its way down as fall settled in, a welcome change from the sweltering heat of the summer. Zengo grabbed his watch off the dresser, careful not to disturb his collection of coins, stacked perfectly by type.

The bathroom was outfitted with the latest high-tech furnishings from his father's home-remodeling company. Zengo brushed his mouth plates, polished his bill, and then opened the vanity mirror, selecting one of the neatly placed bottles of fur product. He squeezed a dab out onto his webbed flipper and with a quick flip of the tufts of his coiffure, he was ready for his day. He smirked at himself in the mirror and thought aloud, "I'm going to be the flyest platypus on the force." He struck a few poses, imagining how he'd look to the bad guys when he took them down.

"Honey," Zengo's mother shouted as he turned down the stairs. "You're going to be late!"

"Ma, I'm already ready."

His mother had his hot chocolate waiting for him in the kitchen, just as she did every morning. "I'm sorry, sweetheart. I just know how much this day means to you. Look! I put your hot chocolate in your favorite mug!"

Zengo looked hard at the clown's face plastered on its side. It used to be his favorite mug. It was the one he got from the Kalamazoo City Circus when he was seven. Sometimes his mom forgot he was a grown platypus. He gave her a hug, and pulled a stainless steel travel mug from the cabinet.

Zengo's dad entered the large, modern kitchen, sweaty and dressed head to webbed toe in running

gear. The morning newspaper sat in a pile on the kitchen table, the crossword puzzle already completed. Zengo glanced at the clock. Seven twenty on the button. His dad was like a machine. He'd been going on the same run every morning for twenty years, and was never more than a minute off.

"Finally up, lazybones? Today's the big day, isn't it?" Zengo's dad toweled himself off as Zengo's mom gave him a glass of ice water. "Shouldn't you get moving? It's your first day on the force, after all. Remember: if you're not fifteen minutes early, you're fifteen minutes late."

"I've got time, Dad; the precinct is only ten minutes away." Zengo tipped the milk to fill his cereal bowl, but poured too much, spilling milk across the counter. "Aw, man!"

"I'll get that, honey." His mom was quick with a sponge, wiping down the counter. "Here, let me."

She poured him a new bowl of Fruity Pops and put it on the table, where wheat toast and a glass of orange juice were waiting. "Sit, dear; you'll need a good meal to start your day."

Zengo chomped away, trying to ignore the commercial that was blaring on the TV. He wished his family would eat a meal in silence for once. To make matters worse, it was the same annoying commercial that had been playing for weeks.

"PANDINI ENTERPRISES," shouted the announcer. "YOUR CITY, BETTER!" Zengo watched pictures of all the Pandini businesses flash past on the screen. "Black and White, the highest-rated restaurant in the southeast according to *D-Vower Magazine;* Bamboo, the hottest club and lounge in the city; Roar, the most state-of-the-art gym and sports training facility in the world; and soon . . . the all-new Kalamazoo Coliseum, home of the Kalamazoo City Sharks!"

Next came the image of Pandini Tower, the tallest and most garish building in the city. Then Frank Pandini Jr. himself, the purveyor of all this wonderfulness, walked onto the screen, flashing his winning smile. He was probably the best-known person in town—thanks to his never-ending television and radio ads, his billboards, and the sports teams he sponsored.

Zengo cringed as Pandini opened his mouth to speak. "HELLO, NEIGHBORS! I'm Frank Pandini and I'm here for you. Remember my motto: YOUR CITY, BETTER! And if I haven't seen you already, I'll be seeing you real soon." Before the commercial ended, Pandini gave a wink to the camera.

Zengo was disgusted. He reached over to the flat screen his dad had installed under the cabinets and snapped it off. "You can't turn around in this town without seeing that panda's mug," he grumbled, sitting back down.

"Now, Ricky, he's done a lot for this city," said Mr. Zengo, as he took a sip of coffee from his Pandini Enterprises–branded cup. "He's brought it back to life. I remember when I married your mom and she

wanted to move back to her hometown, I thought it was the worst idea in the world. This place was a real no-hoper. A dead end."

Zengo had grown up hearing these stories about the bad old days, when crime bosses ran the show and kept honest people from getting ahead. The story was so familiar that he knew, word for word, what his mother would say next.

"If it wasn't for my dear pop, this would be a ghost town," she said, dabbing her eye with the edge of her apron. "He lost his life taking down Frank Pandini Sr."

Zengo slammed his mug down on the table. "That's just it. Why are we all so thrilled about everything that louse's son does? I just don't trust Frank Pandini Jr."

"If 'like father, like son' was true in every case, my boy," laughed Mr. Zengo, patting his fit midriff, "you'd be out running every morning with me and eating fruit salad instead of gorging on junk food."

This was an old routine, too. It was time to change the subject. "I wonder who I'll get for a partner," Zengo said. "I hope he's cool."

Zengo's dad sat back in his chair. "Well, Sergeant Plazinski knows what he's doing. You just listen to him,

Ricky. Keep your head down, and all those detectives are going to be calling you sergeant in a few years! Just like your granddad."

"Actually, he was a lieutenant, dear," said Mrs. Zengo.

Zengo looked at his mom, who smiled at him encouragingly. He ate one more bite of his cereal, downed his juice, and grabbed his travel mug.

"All right, I'm off. Wish me luck, guys!" he said.

"Good luck, honey!" his mother said.

His father raised his cup of coffee. "Do us proud, Ricky."

Zengo stopped in the doorway. "I will, Dad. You'll see."

PLATYPUS POLICE SQUAD HEADQUARTERS, 7:58 A.M.

Platypus Police Squad headquarters was an impressive building, a wide structure made of concrete, glass, and steel. Zengo knew it hadn't always been this way. In his grandfather's day, the precinct was a fraction of the size. They barely had a budget for pencils, let alone the latest in forensic equipment. All that changed the day that Frank Pandini Jr. came back to town. After making his fortune and erecting Pandini Tower, Pandini's first charitable donation went to renovating and expanding the facilities for the Platypus Police Squad. Pandini

bought and
knocked
down the
adjacent
run-down
apartment
buildings,
and donated
the land to
the police. It
was the least
he could do, he said,
considering his father was responsible for so much of
the old Kalamazoo City.

Zengo stopped at the portrait of his grandfather,
Lieutenant Dailey, in the foyer. After giving it a snappy
salute, he turned a corner and ran right into the hustle
and chaos that was Platypus Police Squad headquarters. Cops and detectives and lawyers were running
back and forth across the floor; perps and witnesses
were being shuffled from office to office, cell to cell.
Zengo was overwhelmed by the scene. Maybe he was
even just a little distracted. In any case, his next move
was not fly at all.

"Yeee-OW!" cried the old-timer he had banged into. "Watch where you're going!"

The contents of Zengo's mug were now splattered across the front of the senior detective's shirt. Zengo looked at his mug in horror; he apparently hadn't screwed the top on tightly.

"Aw jeez, oh man. I'm really sorry about that." Zengo attempted to dab the guy's tie with tissues from the nearby desk, but he just smeared around the brown liquid, making the mess worse. He hoped this detective wasn't someone important.

13

"I'm. Covered. In. Coffee!" the old-timer said through gritted teeth. The veins in his forehead were nearly bursting.

"Nah, man. I don't drink coffee; that's hot chocolate." Zengo raised his mug. "Start my day, every day, with a cup of hot chocolate with extra chocolate sauce and a handful of mini marshmallows. Stay right there, let me run and get some paper towels."

"Forget the paper towels, junior. I'll take care of it myself." He stalked away.

"Sorry . . . ," called Zengo to the retreating back. *Not a great way to start off the new job,* he thought to himself. Officers and detectives continued to run past him in a never-ending rush. Where was he supposed to go?

"Are . . . you . . . the . . . new . . . guy?" said a secretary, standing up slowly from her desk. Zengo hadn't even noticed her before.

"Yes, ma'am," said Zengo.

"Go . . . see . . . Sergeant . . .

Plazinski," she said, pointing to a frosted-glass door at the back of headquarters.

Zengo screwed the lid on his travel mug tightly, downed what was left of his hot chocolate, straightened his shirt and jacket, and headed for the sergeant's office.

Sergeant Plazinki opened the door even before Zengo had a chance to knock.

"Rick! Come on in!"

The sarge headed back to his desk, and Zengo shut the door behind him. It was much quieter in here than it was out on the floor. Plazinski motioned for Zengo to take a seat on one of the orange plastic chairs in the middle of the office, while he perched on the corner of his desk. The wall behind him was covered with certificates and awards.

"It's great to have you here," Plazinski said. "Top marks from the academy, dean's list every year . . . You're going to fit right in, my boy. And I've teamed you up with one of our veterans, whose partner just retired. Corey O'Malley's been here for years. Cut his bill back when Pandini Sr. was running this town, back when you couldn't walk the streets in daylight,

let alone at night. He even started out as a beat cop, working under your grandfather."

That sounds promising, Zengo thought. The old pro and the hotshot rookie, teaming up, busting some crime. O'Malley must be one tough guy if he was on the force when Zengo's grandfather was running the show. He wondered how many push-ups he could do.

"Oh, about that, Sergeant," said Zengo in a low tone. "I'm kind of hoping we could keep the fact that I'm Lieutenant Dailey's grandson more or less on the down-low. You know what I mean?"

The sergeant smiled. "Want to make it on your own, son? Not on Lieutenant Dailey's coattails?"

Zengo shrugged, a little embarrassed. "Something like that."

"Sure thing," said the sergeant. "Our little secret. I know how you must feel. Those are some pretty big shoes to fill." He stood up. "Let's go. I'll introduce you to O'Malley. He'll show you the ropes. And it'll be good for him to work with some new blood."

Zengo stood up so quickly he dropped his mug. "Oops," he said as it clattered on the floor.

"Take your time, kid," said the sergeant.

Zengo followed Plazinski, scanning the crowded room for the toughest-looking guys on the force. *I bet O'Malley is built like a brick wall, his neck as solid as a tree trunk*, Zengo thought as they broke off from the main path and approached a desk.

"Corey O'Malley, meet your new partner, Rick Zengo," said Plazinski.

Oh no.

Detective O'Malley swiveled in his chair and locked eyes with Zengo. Zengo couldn't help but stare at the huge hot-chocolate stain that covered his new partner's shirt and tie. Zengo opened his bill, but no words came out.

O'Malley stood up. "Hello, rookie," he said as he waddled over, offering his hand to shake. Zengo took it, standing dumbly. O'Malley gripped his hand so hard, Zengo thought it would snap right off.

There was an empty desk across from O'Malley's. "Here's your station," he said, gesturing toward the recently vacated chair. "Take a seat."

Zengo finally found his tongue. "Sorry again about your clothes, man."

O'Malley laughed, but it sounded a little forced. "I'd need to wash them eventually." He sat back down at his desk and turned to his computer. Zengo wanted to say something else, but didn't know what.

"Good luck, you two," Plazinski said, and left.

Zengo sat in his desk chair and gave it a test swivel. Smooth. He opened each drawer. None of them stuck. Sweet. He beat a little rhythm on the desktop, wondering what would happen next.

Two other guys in plainclothes, probably detectives too, came up to O'Malley's desk. They glanced at Zengo with a combination of curiosity and unfriendliness. But their focus was on O'Malley, still typing on his computer, his back to them.

"Sure gonna miss McGrath, won't ya, O'Malley?" said one.

"Yeah, twenty-five years on the force," said the other. "Who are you going to lean on now to keep

your tail clean?"

O'Malley ignored them.

"I'm talking to you, O'Malley," said the first again.

O'Malley glanced over his shoulder, annoyed. "Diaz? Lucinni? Shouldn't you guys be out heading up the clean-up detail from the police horse parade?"

"Listen, we all knew who carried the weight with you two," sneered Diaz. "Even if it's you who's literally carrying more weight these days." He poked O'Malley in the belly.

"Now there's a new number-one detective partnership on the squad!" said Lucinni.

"Diaz-Lucinni REPRESENT!" they shouted in unison as they high-fived. Then they stood there looking very pleased with themselves.

O'Malley caught Zengo's eye and shook his head.

The secretary who had shown Zengo where Plazinski's office was came slowly around the corner, pushing a mail cart.

"Whatcha got there, Peggy?" asked Diaz.

She pulled out a stack of phone messages and put them on Lucinni's desk. She put another stack on Diaz's desk. They stared at them as Peggy slowly began to speak.

"Lots . . . of . . . folks . . . calling . . . in . . ."

Diaz and Lucinni looked at each other, then back at Peggy, who was gearing up to finish her sentence.

". . . about . . . illegal . . . fish."

Zengo perked up. He loved fish. Herring, especially—it was a bit of a delicacy in Kalamazoo City. His parents picked up some variety of fresh fish every week.

"Bunch of bologna!" said Lucinni, flipping through the messages. "If I had a dollar for everyone who claims to have a lead on illegal fish dealers, I wouldn't need this job." He added the new messages to a huge pile of messages on top of his filing cabinet. "Everyone in this stinkin' town thinks they're experts on stinkin' synthetic fish."

"These . . . people . . . seem . . . very . . . upset," continued Peggy.

"Mackerel, cod, flounder, herring, scallops, haddock... everyone's got a story," added Diaz. "Look, Peggy, we appreciate your concern, but Lucinni here and I have the situation under control. We've been on the case for the last few weeks. We get a ton of calls every day. We get the point. Everyone is getting swindled. If they just patronized the licensed fish retailers, like our PSAs have been telling people to, we wouldn't be wasting our time with these phone calls."

"We've put the word out," said Lucinni. "But everyone thinks they're so smart—they think they can bend the rules and buy fish on the wet market, save a few bucks. If they just listened to us, there wouldn't be any illegal fish in KC."

"Right. So thank you, Peggy, very much"—Diaz slowly took Peggy's hand—"but the next time a call comes in about somebody getting sick because they

ate synthetic fish, stick it in a file somewhere and don't bother us with it. It's taking our attention away from the real crimes of Kalamazoo."

"Ohhhhkay," Peggy said, and slowly turned her cart around. O'Malley got up to help her. When she had finally moved out of earshot, Lucinni muttered, "Someone needs to dust off that relic and bring it to an antique store."

"High five!" said Diaz, and the two slapped webbed flippers.

O'Malley spun around. Even Zengo jumped. "Hey, take all the shots you want at me, but you leave Peggy alone. She was here before you punks even made it to the academy, and she'll be here long after you've retired."

"O'Malley's right," said Zengo. The three of them turned toward him. "I mean, turtles live a really long time."

"O'Malley, you're a little testy this morning," said Lucinni, ignoring Zengo. "Maybe you didn't have your morning doughnut?"

"Or your morning dozen?" asked Diaz, poking O'Malley again.

"Hey, what's that all over your

shirt?" asked Lucinni, as he took O'Malley's tie in his flipper. "Didn't have McGrath around to put your coffee in your sippy cup for you?"

"ALL RIGHT. THAT'S IT." The whole floor stopped and turned as O'Malley stuck his finger in Lucinni's face. "I'm not in the mood for you two monotremes flapping your bills at me!"

"How about me? Can I flap my bill at you, O'Malley?" said Plazinski, suddenly appearing behind them.

Diaz made a slight turn to Lucinni, raised his flipper a half inch, and mouthed, "High five."

"Don't push me, Diaz," the sergeant continued. "You and Lucinni have some cases you should be working on, I assume? Or should I reconsider the mayor's request that we lose two detectives from vice?"

Diaz put his flipper down and made for his desk, with Lucinni close behind.

The sergeant looked at the rest of the floor until everyone got back to work, then turned to O'Malley and Zengo. "We've got a situation out on the docks. Looks like a messy one. I want you two to get on it right away."

Zengo stood up, kicked his chair by accident, and set it spinning across the floor, where it bumped into

the edge of O'Malley's desk, spilling a cup of cold coffee across the morning newspaper.

"Oops," he said, shrugging in apology.

"Let's go, kid," sighed O'Malley, heading for the door.

Zengo tried to mop up some of the coffee, then gave up and hurried after his new partner.

KALAMAZOO CITY STREETS, 11:00 A.M.

Zengo could barely contain his excitement as they drove to the docks. The unmarked squad car was totally sweet. There were sirens and an intercom, and a flashing light could be stuck on the roof with a magnet. The squad car was even outfitted with the most up-to-date laptop. He eyed the police-band radio and the dashboard like it was his birthday party right there in the car. As he was looking at it, the radio crackled to life.

"Car one fifty-three, officers on scene are requesting an update on your position, over."

O'Malley, his eyes on the road, reached for the mouthpiece, but Zengo was quicker.

"That's a big ten-four, Dispatch, car one fifty-three is currently—"

"Give me that," O'Malley said quietly as he snatched the mouthpiece away from Zengo. "Car one fifty-three here, coming up on the coliseum now. We'll be pulling into the shipping area in six minutes." He replaced the handset. "Rule number one, rookie," he said, turning to Zengo. "No one touches the radio but me, got it?"

Zengo slumped down, frustrated. They were probably moving about five miles an hour. He hated being stuck in traffic.

The Kalamazoo Coliseum loomed large up ahead. A huge billboard beside the stadium read:

It's YOUR CHANCE to name the new home of the Kalamazoo City Sharks! A Pandini Project—Your Sharks, Better!

Beside the stadium was a huge construction site where workers were preparing to knock down the old stadium and build the new one.

Zengo rolled his eyes. "Look at that billboard. What

is it with Pandini? I can't get him out of my fur!"

"He's been pretty busy the last year or so," agreed O'Malley. Traffic crawled to an even slower pace.

Compounding the traffic problem, a huge crowd trying to get to the ticket window had spilled out onto the street. "What's up with this?" said Zengo.

"Pandini is selling off parts of the old stadium to raise money for the children's hospital," said O'Malley. "Totally forgot that was happening today."

Zengo scoffed. "Really? A children's hospital?"

"What? You don't think sick kids need medicine? It's a win-win. The hospital gets the funds it needs, and the die-hard baseball fans get a piece of history. And the new stadium is going to be beautiful. I think it's great that our athletes are getting a stadium that they and their fans can be proud of. And the tickets are set to remain cheap. Brings the city together. Time was when the poorer folks and the richer folks lived on opposite sides of the city and didn't intermingle at all." O'Malley stepped on the brakes again to avoid running down an ecstatic fan. "I could do without all the traffic jams from the construction, though."

Now the squad car had stopped completely. Zengo tapped his foot. They were never going to get to the docks. He wished O'Malley would do something.

Or maybe it was up to him.

Zengo slapped the light onto the roof and flipped on the sirens.

The cars in front of them instantly started moving out of the way, and, like a stampeding herd, the crowd outside the coliseum scattered, shoving and knocking one another over.

"WHAT are you DOING, ROOKIE?" shouted O'Malley.

Maybe that wasn't such a good move. Zengo turned off the sirens. "Sorry, partner!" he said. "Thought we were in a hurry is all."

"Rule number one: I'm the senior detective in this

car," said O'Malley. "I say how fast we go, not you. *Especially* when I'm driving."

"I thought rule number one was no one touches the radio but you."

O'Malley turned onto a side road. "Rule number two, we're on a case. We're trying to travel below the radar here. You want everyone in town to know that we're cops? The key is to keep as low a profile as possible. Got it, rookie?"

"Yep," said Zengo.

"Rule number three, and this is where your real education begins, junior: we need to stay tuned in at all times. We watch with our eyes and our ears. We stay focused on the city, listen to its sounds, smell its smells, feel its pulse. We need to know what it's thinking, anticipate what it's about to do next. Detective work is about using your instincts, staying a few steps ahead of the unexpected."

Zengo understood, but there was a problem. "Yeah, I know, but—"

"No buts!" chastised O'Malley. "Detective work is all about keeping your bill to the ground."

"Old lady," said Zengo, his throat tightening.

"What did you just call me?" O'Malley's brows crossed.

"O'Malley, little old lady. There's a—"

"Are you even listening to me, rookie?"

"LITTLE OLD LADY CROSSING THE ROAD! O'MALLEY, WATCH OUT!" Zengo pulled at the wheel, and the detectives swerved just in time.

O'Malley unbuttoned his jacket as his heart rate

quadrupled. "Yowzer. That was a close one!" he said. He glanced in the rearview to see a little old lady shaking her cane.

Zengo folded his arms and smirked. "What was that last bit, about paying attention?"

The radio crackled again. "Where are you, one fifty-three? You're taking all day! What's your ETA?"

"PDQ!" said O'Malley. He flipped the sirens on, threw the light onto the roof, and stepped on the gas. "Rule number four, you gotta know when to put pedal to the metal. They're expecting us at the docks!"

As they finally sped through the streets, Zengo thought, *Sheesh, I would have been there a half hour ago.*

THE DOCKS, 11:28 A.M.

Ten minutes later, Zengo and O'Malley pulled up to the downtown docks. Even during the daytime, the docks were dank and dreary. Dockworkers carried crates off and on boats, and the air was filled with the sounds of distant foghorns. Zengo wasn't used to this, having grown up in the heights, far away from the poorer areas on the east side of Kalamazoo City. He shivered. It seemed ten degrees colder by the water, not to mention the stench! It hit Zengo so hard in the face that he gagged. It was the kind of stink that would linger on his clothes for days. He was starting to wish he hadn't worn his lucky leather jacket.

The easternmost pier was teeming with cops and the forensics team. They all turned as the detectives stepped out of their car. Zengo put on his mirrored sunglasses. It was showtime. Time to solve a crime and show everyone who the new sheriff in KC was.

As they walked toward the group, O'Malley whispered, "Now listen, kid: Don't go saying anything. Don't go touching anything. This is your first crime scene, and these things can get a bit rough. Just follow my lead."

By the time they reached the docks, O'Malley was already out of breath. He led the way to one of the beat cops who was taping off the crime scene on the southeastern pier. "Hey, Casella, what do we got?"

The officer looked up. "Hey, O'Malley," he said, and nodded toward Zengo. "Who's the new kid?"

Zengo took off his sunglasses and smiled brightly. "Detective Rick Zengo."

"My new partner," said O'Malley.

Casella grunted, unimpressed. Zengo reeled his smile back in and offered a friendly nod.

"What's the skinny?" asked O'Malley.

"One of the fishermen found a duffel bag filled with all sorts of fish, most likely of the synthetic variety,

36

early this morning," said Casella. "Some guy's jacket and wallet were left beside it. No money in the wallet, no sign of the guy who owned the jacket, and there are indications things may have gotten violent. If I had to guess, I'd say we're looking at an illegal fish deal gone wrong."

Zengo remembered the conversation at the station that morning about illegal fish. He tried to catch O'Malley's eye, but O'Malley was giving Casella his full attention.

The officer motioned to one of the fishermen who was standing nearby. "This is Peter Freeman," he said. "He's the one who called us."

"Can you walk us down to the crime scene?" O'Malley asked Peter.

"Ayeh," said Peter. "It's over here."

As they followed Peter down past the piers to the crime scene, Zengo leaned over to O'Malley. "What's the deal with illegal fish, anyway?"

Peter stopped in his tracks and pivoted toward Zengo. "I'll tell ya what the deal is with illegal fish. It's puttin' people outta business. People like me, who ah tryin' ta make an honest livin' down here. These bozos who are runnin' around tryin' to make a quick buck are killin' my livelihood." Peter turned and led the detectives down to the crime scene.

"Used to be, herring was rich folks' food," he continued. "We could sell it for top dollah. Not to mention what we could get for fresh salmon and yellowtail. We did okay. Then everyone all over town started to want the top-shelf fish—but nobody was willing to pay for it. That's when this cheap illegal fish started to flood the market. I don't know where these stinkin' fish are from, but I do know they're killin' my business. And these days now, people are startin' to get sick from it. Whoever is makin' this stuff is gettin' sloppy. It used to be a small market, this illegal fish. But I'm tellin' ya, boy, it's everywhere now. And it's even makin' its way into the school, I hear. My kid goes to Kal East, and says every kid in school is eating fish now, even the vegetarians. It's all the rage. If that's the case, it can't all be legal. And someone, somewhere is makin' serious dough off this. Somebody oughta do somethin' about it."

The detectives followed Peter down a long alley that was zigzagged with black tire tracks. Zengo's heart was heavy with the thought of what might have happened here the night before. He nearly walked on the tracks, but O'Malley took ahold of his elbow and led him back to the unmarked pavement. "Watch your tail, kid!" he whispered. "We don't want to compromise any of the evidence."

At the end of the alley, they came upon some battered wooden crates. Peter lifted the lid off of one of them. "We were movin' some supplies off and on the boats and found this." Peter motioned to the open crate. Zengo peered in.

As if the smells on the docks couldn't get any worse, the pungent air that wafted from the wooden box nearly knocked him on his tail. O'Malley took a handkerchief from his back pocket and reached inside the wooden box. He lifted out a shabby jacket, holding it at arm's length.

"Looks like somebody could use a trip to the dry cleaner's," he said.

"Or an appointment with a stylist," muttered Zengo. The tweed jacket had patches on the elbows.

O'Malley turned it around and showed Zengo the back, which was covered with black tire tracks. Zengo could taste the vomit at the back of his mouth and swallowed hard. O'Malley draped the coat over the side of the crate as they continued their examination.

Zengo looked inside the wooden box and saw the source of the odor. It was a blue duffel bag stuffed to the brim with rotting fish. Peter looked to both detectives. "I saw all the fish, figured it was illegal. That's just somethin' I don't mess with. That's why I called you guys."

"You did the right thing," said Zengo. "It's better to leave the handling of illegal fish to the authorities."

O'Malley cleared his throat and said, "Let's wait until forensics takes a look to confirm that this fish is indeed of the illegal variety."

Was he off his rocker? Zengo looked at O'Malley. "Dude, this fish is totally artificial!" he said through the corner of his mouth. "Who would carry around the good stuff in a duffel bag?" He winced. The stench was making him ill.

"Procedures are in place for a reason," said O'Malley. His voice was firm. "Until forensics can prove it for sure, we operate under the assumption that it's *likely* illegal fish. Got it?" O'Malley turned to Peter. "Thank you for your help, sir."

"You bet. Lemme know if you guys need anythin' else," said Peter, with a nod of his head as he shuffled back to the loading area.

"We won't hesitate to be in touch," called Zengo after him. O'Malley glanced over, then pulled a pair of rubber gloves out of his pocket and snapped them on.

"Ordinarily a nasty task like this goes to the junior detective," he said as he reached into the duffel bag to pull out a stinking, rotten fish. "But I figured, it's your first day and all, don't want to make you blow lunch before you even get a chance to eat it." He smiled. The fish's head slid off and fell to the ground, bouncing at Zengo's feet.

"Thanks, man," said Zengo, shuffling his feet, but he couldn't help but notice that O'Malley wasn't letting him do any of the work.

While O'Malley bagged the sample for forensics, Zengo moved away and took a few cleansing breaths. Then he stepped back to the crate, forcing himself to ignore the stench. He wanted to get a closer look at the duffel bag.

It had a logo on the side that was mostly rubbed off. It looked to Zengo like some kind of monster, or jungle cat. Whatever it was supposed to be, it had fangs and didn't look friendly. Was it some sort of gang emblem?

O'Malley picked up the jacket again. He pulled a well-worn wallet out of the breast pocket and inspected its contents. When O'Malley pulled out a driver's license, his bill dropped.

"What is it?" asked Zengo. "Let me see." Zengo peered over O'Malley's shoulder and studied the license. There was nothing out of the ordinary about the guy in the photograph. Just a dorky-looking fellow with glasses. "You know this guy? William Hopkins?"

"I don't. But my kids do. He's a teacher over at East

Kalamazoo High School." O'Malley handed the card to Zengo. "One of my kids has him for English."

Zengo inspected the license. "A teacher dealing illegal fish?"

"He's innocent until proven guilty, slugger."

Zengo scowled—*That's what you call a little kid*, he thought—but turned back to study the driver's license. The teacher lived on Maple Ridge Lane, a nice little gated community in the better part of town, only a few blocks from where Zengo lived, and a long drive from Kal East. Zengo paused to consider that O'Malley probably lived over on the east side.

"Let's see what else we can find." O'Malley emptied out the contents of Hopkins's wallet like he was dealing a hand of blackjack. "Organic grocery store rewards card, Master Credit card, Universal Cash card, Kalamazoo City Library card . . ." O'Malley continued to rummage through the wallet and pulled out a small piece of paper. He unfolded it gingerly. It was an ATM receipt. "Looks like Hopkins here just took out a considerable amount of cash. Five hundred bucks." He handed the receipt over to Zengo, who noted the address. "But where'd the cash go? He doesn't have a single buck in his wallet."

"I'd say it's in this bag." Zengo shook the duffel. The illegal fish wiggled like gelatin. "Maybe Teach wasn't a seller but a buyer."

O'Malley pulled a napkin out of Hopkins's wallet and placed it on the crate and continued to search for clues.

Zengo spotted the tossed-aside napkin and stood motionless. The signature color, font, and logo could not be mistaken. "The professor liked the nightlife, huh?"

"What do you mean?"

YOUR CITY BETTER

A PANDINI ENTERP PROJECT

BAMBO

Zengo held the napkin up to his partner. "Bamboo. Only the hottest club in town. All the cool kids hang out there. Best root beer floats in Kalamazoo City. Funny, I figured they had a strict no-dweeb dress code. You know who owns that club don't you?"

"Let me guess," said O'Malley, gazing upward. "Santa Claus?"

Zengo smiled, and followed O'Malley's gaze up to another massive Pandini billboard. "Bingo."

Sanchez, the lead forensics investigator, made his way past the piers and joined the detectives. "Looks like we've got a case of hit-and-run here."

"That's what I think too," said O'Malley. "We also found this duffel bag. It's filled with fish." He waved the plastic sample bag. "I've bagged one for you to take downtown to run some tests. Might be of the illegal variety."

Sanchez peered into the duffel, rubbed off a couple scales, and said, "Oh that is most definitely illegal fish, no question there."

Zengo winked at O'Malley, who quickly changed the subject. "So, what do you make of these tire tracks?"

Sanchez got down on his flippers and knees, hovering just an inch over the burned rubber. "I'd say they were made sometime after midnight. The tracks are still fresh. It looks like whoever the perp was launched the attack from over there." Sanchez pointed to the abandoned packing warehouse at the top of the hill. The business looked as if it hadn't been in operation for at least a decade. Zengo shuddered again. How could this place be part of the same city he lived in?

With his foreflipper, Sanchez tracked the path that the car must have taken. The path ended at the water's edge. "What I don't understand is, the tracks end right here, at the end of the dock. Either somebody stopped on a dime, or we're going to be fishing a car out of the bay."

"Let's take a look," said O'Malley, stepping to the edge of the pier and kneeling down. He looked back at Zengo. "You coming?"

Zengo had been hanging back near the crates, pretending to be very busy with the evidence. He had been hoping O'Malley wouldn't notice. Zengo couldn't swim. In fact, he was afraid of water. Not a proud thing for a platypus to admit. "I'll be over there in a second," he said, his head in the crate. "Just checking something here."

"No sweat," said O'Malley. "I'll take a look, then." He took off his suit coat and his sunglasses, rolled up both sleeves, knelt by the water's edge, and plunged his head into the murky drink.

Zengo was startled by a sudden flash to his left. It was a reporter with a camera.

O'Malley pulled his head out of the water. "Nothing there," he said. Then he noticed the reporter. "Doherty, what are you doing here?" His tone was the opposite of friendly.

"Sorry, fellas," said Doherty. "I hope I'm not interrupting anything. Just got a coupla questions. . . ." Doherty took out a notebook and started scribbling a few observations.

"Who gave you clearance to walk past the caution tape?" O'Malley asked. "This is a crime scene. Now get out of here before I break that camera in two!"

"I'll take care of him," said Zengo as he escorted Doherty aside. The last thing Zengo wanted was to end up in the papers because his partner flew off the handle.

"All right. Hope you're not afraid of reptiles, too!" O'Malley barked before walking back to their car.

Zengo stopped for a moment and let out an audible sigh. So what if O'Malley had picked up on Zengo's

fear of water? Zengo decided to see if he could make a connection with this sneaky little reporter. He might turn out to be a handy contact at some point. Besides, how proud would his mom be if he got his picture in the paper, especially on his very first day on the job? Standing tall, he posed while Doherty snapped.

"Remember, the Platypus Police Squad will not stand for illegal herring in this city," said Zengo. "Kalamazoo's finest is on it, and we'll be putting a stop to this nonsense."

"I'm all over this illegal herring story," said Doherty. "This situation stinks."

"You got that right," said Zengo. He pulled out a pad of paper and a pen. "If you ever come up with an angle that might help us, here's my email address."

"Thanks," said Doherty, pocketing the information.

"And . . . maybe you could email me a few of those photos too?" said Zengo, flashing a big smile.

"No sweat," said Doherty, scuttling away.

Zengo hurried back to the squad car before O'Malley noticed he had still been talking to Doherty. Amid the commotion of officers collecting evidence and dock-workers moving freight, he spotted someone lurking behind a lamppost by the abandoned warehouse. The shadowy figure seemed out of place. What was he doing there?

Zengo got back to the car and got inside as O'Malley was opening the trunk, grabbing a towel and a package of chocolate cupcakes. He offered one to Zengo, who was about to reach for it until he remembered his father giving him a hard time that morning about his diet. "No thanks, I'm good," he said.

The radio crackled. "O'Malley, come in." It was Sergeant Plazinski. O'Malley wiped the crumbs off his bill and reached in through the open driver's-side window and answered. Zengo leaned over to listen in on the conversation.

"Yes sir, Sergeant." O'Malley stood up straight.

"What's going on down there?" Even over the radio, Plazinzki's voice commanded respect.

O'Malley brought Plazinski up to speed on what they had found: the duffel, the wallet, the napkin from Bamboo.

"I've heard of Bamboo," said Plazinski. "That's Frank Pandini's new place."

O'Malley put his flipper on his hip. "Yeah, apparently he's in the nightclub business now."

"Pandini's in any business he wants to be in. But Bamboo is pretty hip for a guy like Hopkins."

"You knew the professor?"

"I'm the sergeant, O'Malley. This is my city. Hopkins has won Teacher of the Year more than a few times. You know how many of those boring ceremonies I've had to sit through? Hold on a second while I plug Hopkins's name into the system."

Over the radio came the sound of Plazinski tapping away at his keyboard. There was silence for a moment and then, "Hmmph!"

"What's up?" said O'Malley.

"Looks like somebody filed a missing-persons report on Hopkins yesterday. Turns out he hadn't shown up for class for the past week and a half. No

51

calls, no notice, no nothing."

"That doesn't sound like the behavior of an award-winning teacher," said Zengo.

"Sure doesn't," said Plazinski. "I'll send a few blue-and-whites over to his house to see if they can come up with anything. Priority number one is to find out what happened to this guy. Start with the club, Bamboo, as soon as it opens. Could be that's the last place anyone saw him. See what you can dig up. But O'Malley—don't put your foot in anything over there. Keep things civil. There are a million reasons why that napkin could have been in the professor's pocket, and we don't want to ruffle any feathers. Or fur, as the case may be."

"Yes, sir," said O'Malley.

"Bring Zengo with you. This is the perfect chance for the rookie to see how things are done in the big leagues. Oh, and O'Malley . . ."

"Yes, sir."

"It's not even noon yet. Put the chocolate cupcakes away."

Zengo smirked as O'Malley stuffed the cupcake into his pocket. "Yes, sir."

"Now get going. I want an update by the end of the day."

"Ten-four." O'Malley got into the car and put the radio back on the console.

As the car rumbled to a start, Zengo looked back toward the lamppost. "Say, O'Malley, didn't the crowds get dispersed?"

"Yeah, why?"

Zengo scanned the scene around the warehouse, but the shadowy figure was gone. "Never mind."

EAST KALAMAZOO MIDDLE/HIGH SCHOOL, 12:25 P.M.

Car 153 headed east, away from the docks. "Isn't Bamboo north of here?" asked Zengo.

"Hope you don't mind, I'm taking a quick detour," said O'Malley.

"Where to?"

"To pick up my kids. It's a half day today."

O'Malley turned in to Sixteenth Street to find a traffic jam stretching out for blocks. Zengo got out of the car to get a better view of the situation. A block ahead he saw several gigantic cement mixers jamming the road at the entrance to the school. The lawn was a mess of activity. Construction workers ran back and forth from the school to a series of trailers set up across the street. A fifty-foot crane was approaching the school from Tenth Avenue. Wood and bricks and cement sat in massive piles everywhere. And above all of it hung a big banner that read: A PANDINI PROJECT— YOUR SCHOOL, BETTER!

"Is this guy *everywhere*?" said Zengo, getting back into the car.

"He's building a new science wing," said O'Malley. "The school sure could use it."

There was even more construction going on across the street. "What's that?" said Zengo.

"That's the new football stadium," said O'Malley.

"Let me guess," said Zengo. "Pandini?"

"You got it," said O'Malley. He pointed to a billboard above the stadium construction. It showed Frank Pandini standing above a miniature model of the new school layout, flashing his famous Pandini smile.

"The kids are pretty excited about the stadium," said

STADIUM OPENING FOR THE BIG GAME THIS FRIDAY NIGHT!

Your Kal East Football, BETTER!

O'Malley. "I kind of am, too, I've got to admit. There was nothing like this here back when I went to East."

Zengo studied Pandini's billboard. It was impressive, but Zengo couldn't shake the feeling that it made Pandini look like a giant fire-breathing monster about to destroy the city.

One of the cement mixers finally got out of the road, and the cars started moving. Two kids had been standing behind it, and they waved to the squad car.

O'Malley rolled down the window. "Hop in the back, boys," he said. "Where's Vanessa?"

The boys got into the backseat and immediately slid down below the windows. "She's going to that new club with her friends," said the older one.

"Bamboo?" asked O'Malley.

"That's the one."

Zengo and O'Malley shared a look.

"Figures," said O'Malley. "Boys, say hi to my new partner, Detective Zengo. Zengo, the big fella is Johnny—"

"Ugh! Dad, how many times do I have to tell you? I go by Jonathan now. Johnny is a name for babies and I'm in high school." Jonathan shot his dad a look in the rearview and then slumped down again as another group of kids walked by.

"Oh. Right. Sorry. Jonathan. And the little fella is Declan. I guess you won't be meeting my oldest, Vanessa."

Zengo turned around and waved. The boys smiled. "Cool jacket!" said Declan, looking up from his game.

"Thanks, buddy. It's my lucky one."

"I've always wanted a leather jacket, but the only jackets I've ever had are his old ones." He stuck a thumb out at Jonathan.

Zengo glanced down at his leather jacket, unsure how to respond. Jonathan looked like he was about to say something, but a group of kids passed by and he and Declan slunk still farther down in their seats.

"How come you were waiting so far away from the main entrance?" asked O'Malley.

"Dad, you know why," said Jonathan, waving his arm as if he were throwing something.

"Oh, come on," cried O'Malley. "You're still embarrassed by Career Day when you were in fourth grade? Who even remembers that?"

"Dad, you shot out a window with your boomerang," said Declan.

"Girls still snicker when they pass me in the halls," said Jonathan.

Zengo laughed. "Is that true?"

Jonathan and Declan both nodded in unison.

"I thought the window was open!" said O'Malley. "Rule number one: give your dad a break for once."

The traffic moved down the block, and the facade of the new football stadium was visible past a row of trees. The crane moved toward it, and men started securing the hook to the statue of the Kal East Fighting Pirate.

"Are they replacing the Fighting Pirate statue too?" asked O'Malley. "They've had that statue there since I was a kid!"

"We're getting a new mascot," said Declan.

"Don't tell me, let me guess," said Zengo. "It's a panda, right?"

"That's it," said Declan. "We're the Fighting Pandas now."

Zengo glared sideways at O'Malley before he leaned out the window to get a better look. Just then, something flashed in front of the car. O'Malley slammed his foot on the brake, which caused Zengo to bang his head on the window frame. Zengo rubbed his noggin and saw that some kid had run right out into the road. Now he was standing in the street, staring at them and looking scared out of his wits. He was tall and dressed in designer clothes from foot to muzzle, with a Kal East varsity jacket slung over his shoulder. Zengo stared hard. He had seen this kid before. Down at the docks.

"Dad! You almost ran over the quarterback!" Declan shouted.

O'Malley honked. "I didn't almost do anything—he bolted out in front of me."

"You'll want to be careful, Dad," said Jonathan. "That's Blake Cameron. He's only about the coolest kid in the whole school, and his parents are loaded. Oh, and one more thing . . ."

Blake finally snapped out of it and waved sheepishly at them. He held out his paw behind him, and someone took it and crossed the road with him.

"Vanessa!" said O'Malley.

"He's Vanessa's new boyfriend," said Jonathan.

Cars were honking behind them as they watched Vanessa and Blake head toward the school parking lot. It looked like Vanessa was pretending she didn't see them. Probably standard operating procedure for all of O'Malley's kids, thought Zengo, remembering how his parents sometimes embarrassed him. But what was she doing with that guy from the docks?

"Well, quarterback or not, he won't be able to win many games if he keeps walking in front of cars."

"He won't be able to play many games if he doesn't pass his classes," said Jonathan.

"He's in my English class, which he's just about flunking, and I hear he's not doing too well in his other classes, either."

"Swell," said O'Malley as they pulled out of the parking lot and back onto Sixteenth Street. "Great boyfriend."

"Don't worry, Dad," said Declan. "If he messes with her, I'll knock his block off."

"Good luck reaching his block, squirt," said Jonathan as he ruffled his little brother's hair.

They drove into a modest older residential neighborhood. The houses were built pretty close together. They were so small, they made Zengo's house seem like a mansion by comparison. O'Malley pulled to a stop before a two-story job with a chain-link fence, behind which Zengo could see a neatly tended flower garden.

"Have a good afternoon, boys," said O'Malley. "Help your mother, okay?"

"Sure thing, Dad," Declan said as they got out.

"So long, Detective Zengo," said Jonathan.

Zengo waved. "Later, guys." He turned to O'Malley. "Nice kids," he said.

O'Malley smiled. "They're okay. Their big sister is a piece of work, though."

"That reminds me," said Zengo. "I think I've seen that kid Blake before."

"That doesn't surprise me," said O'Malley. "Him being a football hero and all."

"No, it's not that," said Zengo. "I think I saw him this morning. At the dock."

O'Malley glanced his way for a moment, then turned back to the road. "Really?"

"Pretty sure," said Zengo. "He was slinking around down by the warehouse. Are you thinking what I'm thinking?"

"If you're thinking that the kid failing English showing up at the missing English teacher's crime scene might be a little more than a coincidence," said O'Malley, "then yes, I'm thinking exactly what you're thinking."

"Looks like we have two reasons to check out Bamboo," said Zengo, flipping on the siren. "Let's step on it!"

O'Malley flipped it off. "Rule number one, kid, remember?"

BAMBOO, 1:13 P.M.

Zengo stared out the window, watching the passing skyscrapers tower overhead, while O'Malley merged onto the inner-loop beltway. A huge billboard loomed over the highway. For once, it wasn't for a Pandini project. It advertised a defense lawyer, Doug Raskin, and his "One hundred percent acquittal rate—guaranteed!"

Traffic was crawling at a snail's pace again because of construction. *Our city, slower*, Zengo thought.

O'Malley must have been thinking about Pandini too. "Listen, Zengo, when we get to this club, we keep a low profile," he said.

"Why?" asked Zengo. "Don't want to upset the town hero? Pandini might not be breaking any laws, but he clearly doesn't care who he's got to step on to get what he wants."

"Hey now, let's not throw an accusation like that around so loosely."

"Come on, O'Malley, do you really believe this character is what everyone says he is? Anyone who advertises his good deeds as much as this guy does must be up to something."

"Pandini's done a great deal of good in this city." O'Malley threw on the blinkers and changed lanes. "Sometimes the apple does fall far from the tree."

Zengo was unconvinced. "You were on the squad when Pandini's father was taken down, weren't you?"

O'Malley nodded curtly. "I was one of the guys on the special force assigned to Pandini's dad when he was the city's biggest crime boss. Kalamazoo was a cesspool back then. Frank Senior ruled this city with an iron fist. But the PPS watched his every move. We knew that a guy that big, with his paws in so many honey pots, was bound to misstep. He went down hard. And we've been cleaning up his mess ever since."

"My gut says the Pandinis have more in common than most people are willing to admit," said Zengo.

O'Malley shrugged his shoulders. "Sure, Pandini is as ambitious as his dad was. But he was just a kid when his father got sent off to Grayson Prison. Frank Junior was left with nothing, shipped out to Branbury Prep, got himself a good education, and went off to make his money the hard way—through honest work."

"I know, I've seen the commercials."

O'Malley swerved in and out of traffic. "We're lucky enough Pandini returned to his hometown to share his success. The billboards are all a bit much, but he's positioning Kalamazoo to be a first-class city."

Zengo started poking around on the radio. Why was this car ride taking so long?

"Anyway," said O'Malley, "until we find out otherwise, I recommend we operate under the assumption that Pandini is playing by the books. No matter what we think of his billboards or his motives, Pandini has gotten to be in very tight with all the muckety-mucks in city hall, not to mention Sergeant Plazinski. Rule number one: when it comes to Pandini, it's best to button your lip."

Zengo could hear the warning in his partner's voice.

But he wasn't persuaded. "I hear you," he said. "But I just can't believe how quickly people forget what his father did."

"Don't worry, rookie. Not everyone has forgotten." Something passed over O'Malley's face. "Oh crud, this is our exit!"

Zengo clutched the passenger-side door as O'Malley veered across three lanes. When the car finally straightened out, the skyscrapers in the side-view mirror receded as the sprawling upscale business complexes rose up ahead.

"Not sure who's a bigger threat to society there, partner!" said Zengo, straightening his shirt and jacket.

"Can it, rookie."

They drove past designer condos and overpriced coffee shops and pulled into the Bamboo parking lot. It fit in perfectly with the rest of the Pandini development around it: all dark tinted glass, with fake black-and-white palm trees decorating the entryway.

"Remember," said O'Malley. "Keep a low profile. I'll do the talking in here, okay?"

"Yeah, I get it." Zengo threw his door open. He was

tired of everyone tiptoeing around Pandini, and he had had about enough of being treated like a little kid.

It was only midday, but the parking lot was nearly full. There were rows upon rows of flashy cars, some representing an entire year's salary for a normal person.

If Zengo had a weakness, it was flashy cars. "What do you think, O'Malley?" he said, practically drooling as he looked at all the shiny, cool, expensive machinery. "When do we get to ride around in one of these?"

O'Malley climbed out of the beat-up squad car and shut the door. "I don't think the sarge has it in his budget, but maybe Pandini will make a donation-in-kind to the force."

Zengo caressed the shiny chrome and sparkling rims of each car they passed. "See, I told you this place was upscale," he said. "Given the clientele, I'm even more curious to find out what Hopkins was doing here." Zengo stopped at a shiny red two-seater convertible. "O'Malley, look at this."

O'Malley kept walking. "To be honest with you, kid, I couldn't care less about fancy cars."

"Even ones that might be owned by your daughter's boyfriend?" O'Malley turned to Zengo, who was squatting next to a license plate that read QB.

The detectives stepped into the club. It was dimly lit, but it was as posh as Zengo expected it to be. Granite countertops, red-velvet curtains—this place oozed money. A live band jammed onstage. They were loud, ear-piercingly loud. A chick belted out a tune, or something that could nearly pass as a tune, into the microphone. O'Malley muttered to Zengo, "That bird's squawking could make a guy go deaf. Guess there's no audition process to sing at Pandini's establishments."

"That's Roxie Lane," said Zengo. "The hottest pop star in Kalamazoo City."

A bouncer who was as big as a house stepped into

their path. "Don't see many people your age here," he said to O'Malley, who smiled uneasily.

Zengo reached into his jacket to pull out his badge, but O'Malley nudged him. "We just came here to check out the root beer floats," O'Malley said. "They've been getting rave reviews."

The bouncer didn't look too happy to let them pass. He finally stepped aside, but not without a hard look of steely-eyed menace.

Zengo scanned the crowd. Kids, mostly, and lots of them, including Vanessa, who was dancing with ome friends. O'Malley didn't seem to notice her, and Zengo decided to leave it that way. He didn't see Blake anywhere, but that didn't mean that he wasn't on the premises. For now, thought Zengo, he had bigger fish to fry.

The tables were all full of kids drinking root beer floats and eating mile-high plates of fish. Just about every color in the rainbow was represented. "Popular delicacies," said Zengo. "Wonder if any of it's legal?"

O'Malley pointed to the chalkboard that read: SPECIAL TODAY: FRESH HERRING. $14.99. "At that price, it better be," he said.

O'Malley and Zengo moseyed up to the bar and took two stools. The bartender was busy pouring root beer floats. "What can I get you?" he asked without looking up from his pour.

"Just a few answers, please," said O'Malley. "We're looking for a guy who might have been in here last night. Do you recognize him?" O'Malley held up a copy of Hopkins's license photo.

The bartender barely glanced at it. "Ain't seen him." He plopped in scoops of ice cream and placed the floats on a tray, which was quickly snatched up by a waitress.

Zengo wasn't buying it. "Let's try this again," he said. "This guy was in here last night. What can you tell us about him?"

O'Malley cut in quickly. "Hey, if he didn't see him, he didn't see him."

Zengo ignored his partner's lead and continued to grill the bartender. "Surely somebody here saw this guy. Maybe there was another bartender slinging drinks last night?"

The bartender stopped cold and turned to Zengo. "I'm the only bartender here. My job is to serve the best root beer floats in town. My job isn't to take attendance. But I'm telling you, I didn't see your guy in here. Not last night. Not ever."

Zengo flashed his badge. "Maybe this will help jog your memory," he said.

The bartender smirked, and didn't miss a beat. "Sorry, I got nothing for you," he said, turning his back on the detectives.

O'Malley shook his head slightly. Zengo looked

down, embarrassed. Pulling his badge was a stupid move. Any chance they had of flying under the radar was blown. Now a skinny little busboy collecting dirty dishes behind the bar was glaring at him. Zengo glared right back. "You got a problem?" he asked.

"Yeah, I do. You're my problem, monotreme," snapped the busboy. "If ol' Carpy here says he didn't see nobody, he didn't see nobody. There's nothing fishy goin' on here, so why don't you just move along."

Zengo leaned over the bar and asked through gritted teeth, "What's that supposed to mean?"

In one leap, the busboy was over the bar and in Zengo's face.

The music stopped, and everyone at the club was staring over at the scuffle. The bartender ran around the bar and pulled his busboy back by the tail. "Joey, leave 'em be! Get these dishes to the kitchen."

O'Malley grabbed Zengo by the collar of his leather jacket. "Let's get out of here," he hissed.

Just then, the front door swung open and daylight pierced the room. The air shifted. The music stopped, and the hum of the crowd hushed.

Frank Pandini stood in the doorway, his wide frame silhouetted momentarily by the light from outside. It was only lunchtime, but Pandini was dressed in his white tuxedo. Even Zengo was speechless.

Pandini greeted his patrons at each table. His handshakes were reinforced with confident shoulder pats. His smile, clearly a perfected skill, lit up even this darkest of rooms. After a moment, the bouncer lumbered over to greet his boss and whispered in his ear.

Pandini approached as the busboy hopped behind the bar to snatch up his bin of dirty dishes. "I under-stand we have two of the city's finest in our presence." He placed a paw on each of the detectives' shoulders. "Please accept my apologies for the rash behavior of my staff." Pandini glared at Joey and motioned to Zengo and O'Malley to sit. "Please, have a seat."

O'Malley accepted the offer, but Zengo remained standing, taking a spot behind O'Malley, his arms folded, his face fixed in a cold stare.

"Suit yourself, Detective." Pandini smiled. "Now, I understand you're not just here to enjoy the floats."

O'Malley shot Zengo a look to make clear he would be taking the lead. "We're looking for information about a missing person. We have reason to believe he was here at your club just last evening." O'Malley

offered the photo of Hopkins. Pandini took a look, but shook his head.

"Sorry, never seen him."

"Well, we found a Bamboo napkin in his jacket. And we were just trying to put together a few pieces—"

"I'm going to go ahead and stop you right there, Detective. Somebody lost his jacket? We have a lost-and-found at the coatroom. Bobby will be happy to help you—"

"The jacket was found down on the docks, in a crate of illegal fish."

Pandini took this in. "If you're insinuating that the illegal fish you found has anything to do with my club, I can assure you that I have a zero-tolerance policy for such subversive behavior in my establishments. Illegal fish is a scourge, and must be eradicated."

Zengo caught a glimpse of Joey, who was busing tables across the room, but still glaring at the detectives. Zengo snarled back. Pandini caught the look.

"What's the matter with you, Detective?" he asked. "Indigestion?"

"Yeah, indigestion from all this malarkey you're feeding us," said Zengo. "We think Hopkins was in here and he was in here yesterday. The professor pulled money from the ATM next door. Why would he bother pulling money from that ATM when he teaches on the east side of town and lives nowhere near here?"

Zengo was playing a dangerous game and he knew it. O'Malley glared at him, but Zengo couldn't stop now. "Why would Hopkins go so out of the way on his commute to stop here for cash?"

Pandini flashed his million-dollar smile. "That's an excellent question. But the only person who could answer that for you would be the good professor himself. If the professor was one of my many employees, I'd be able to help you—they're under my surveillance day and night. I can tell you what they eat for lunch, what brand of toothpaste they use, and the names of their favorite teachers in elementary school. But the professor wasn't one of my employees, so I don't know anything about him. Any information on the whereabouts of the missing professor is not for me to collect."

Pandini turned to his bartender. "Carpy, did you see the professor in here last night?"

"I ain't seen him, Frank."

Pandini stood and loomed over Zengo. "If Carpy didn't see him, nobody saw him. Now, I'd appreciate it if you'd stop questioning my employees, as we've disrupted the lunch crowd enough. Carpy, two root beer floats for the detectives, on the house. Make sure you put some extra sugarcane in them. These boys deserve our gratitude for their fine work."

"My apologies for any inconvenience," O'Malley said quickly. "My partner here is new on the force, and I hope you can forgive his—"

Zengo didn't want to hear any more. He stomped toward the door and waited outside for O'Malley, pacing furiously in the parking lot.

A moment later, O'Malley charged out the door and right up to Zengo. "What the heck were you thinking back there?"

Zengo was caught off guard. He didn't know O'Malley could get this fired up. But he recovered quickly. "I was thinking, 'Hmmm. Maybe I should do my job.'"

"You're going to get us thrown off this case, if not off the force completely, kid."

"That bartender knows something, O'Malley, I guarantee it."

"Even if I believed you, that matters for nothing if we can't get him to talk. Rule number one: you've got to be patient. You can't just go into a situation like that all boomerangs a-blazing. You need a plan. You need to get the witnesses on your side. You need finesse—"

"I couldn't believe you were just sitting there drooling over the root beer floats and letting Pandini roll all over you. You've lost your edge, old man."

If O'Malley was offended by what Zengo said, he didn't show it. "Slow down, rookie. You're moving way too fast."

"And we don't have time to work at a snail's pace."

"Ahem!" A family of snails scurried past. The father shot Zengo a disgusted look.

Zengo nodded and raised his hand. "Sorry 'bout that."

O'Malley snapped Zengo back to the situation. "Hey! Listen to me. I know you're used to getting your way, but you can't just order people around in situations like this and expect them to cooperate."

Zengo was struck speechless for a moment. "What's that supposed to mean?"

"Look, our number one job right now is to find Hopkins. And thanks to your handiwork, we can cross everyone in Bamboo right off our list of possible informants. Nobody in there will talk to us now, not after what they just saw. We're back to square one."

Zengo opened his bill to keep arguing, but had nothing left to say. Maybe he had jumped in too fast back in Bamboo. He hung his head, but when he looked up, he saw O'Malley gazing across the parking lot.

"Well, you're not a total loss as a detective," said O'Malley. "You really think that's the ATM Hopkins used last night?"

Zengo looked over where O'Malley was pointing. He took a deep breath. "Yeah. The address on the receipt we found matches up."

"In that case, we should be able to get some good information from the surveillance camera, don't you think?"

The old guy had a point, Zengo had to admit.

"There's more than one way to trap a panda," said O'Malley, a smile creeping onto his face. "C'mon, rookie. Let's get going."

Zengo smiled weakly, and nodded.

ZENGO'S HOUSE, 6:30 P.M.

Zengo crossed the threshold as if he had just ran a marathon. It had been a very long day. Zengo's parents had already eaten, but his mother had kept his dinner warm and rushed to get it on the table when she heard the door open. Unfortunately, Zengo's appetite just wasn't there. He slumped down in the leather couch in the living room. His bones were barely rested when his mom and dad swooped in.

"How was it, honey?" his mother asked as she ruffled the top of his head.

"It was all right," he offered, his eyes slightly glazed over.

"All right? Kiddo, this was the day we've all been waiting for," barked his dad. "We want to hear all about it. How's your partner? What did the day bring?

Any action? And most importantly—what did you learn today? If you go through a day without learning, you go through a day without living."

"It was a busy day, Dad. My partner's okay, I guess. Corey O'Malley."

Zengo's dad took a moment, but shook his head. "Sounds vaguely familiar, but I can't place the name. I wonder if he knew your grandpa."

"He's been on the force awhile."

"Sounds like a cop with experience," said Zengo's mom. "You listen to what he has to say and watch what he does. He'll teach you a lot. I know Plazinski would only pair you with one of the best."

Zengo's dad looked at his watch. "Oh jeepers! I'm already running a few minutes late for my Pilates." He kissed Mrs. Zengo and was out the door.

Zengo's mom sat down next to him and patted his flipper. "Hard work, huh?" she said.

"I guess I thought things would go more quickly," he said. "O'Malley says I have to learn to slow down. I think he works at a glacial pace."

"Maybe you two will find a way to meet somewhere in the middle," said Zengo's mom. "Being a good partner means compromising, sometimes."

As she got up and started walking toward the kitchen, Zengo said, "Mom, did I only get this job as a detective because of Grandpa? Or because we're well-off?"

Mrs. Zengo stopped and turned. "Of course not, sweetie! You worked harder than anyone getting through the academy. What makes you say that?"

"No reason."

Zengo was still sitting slumped in his chair when his mother came back a moment later. She put a bowl under his bill. "Honey, I made brownies and saved you the bowl to lick!" She smiled kindly.

"Thanks, Ma. But I'm a grown platypus now; that's kids' stuff."

"Okay, sweetie, I'll just leave it on the kitchen counter then." As she turned to leave, she said, "Whatever you're worried about, your father and I are both very proud of you. You've worked so hard." She leaned over, kissed him on the forehead, and retired for the evening.

Zengo sat alone with his thoughts. He looked over at the glass case in the corner of the living room, which was filled with his dad's civic awards and awards his grandfather had earned in his years on the

Platypus Police Squad. He replayed the day's events in his mind.

The bowl of brownie mix stared at him from the kitchen counter. Zengo lifted himself up from the chair, grabbed the mixing bowl, and licked it clean.

PLATYPUS POLICE SQUAD HEADQUARTERS, 8:10 A.M.

It was another busy morning at Platypus Police Squad headquarters. The night shift had filed their paperwork and left for the day, while the morning shift had already had their briefings and were out patrolling the streets. Most of the detectives were at their desks—following leads, connecting the dots between the whos, the wheres, and the whys.

Zengo was at work early, waiting for his partner. Finally, he spotted O'Malley's car pulling into the parking lot. Zengo walked over to the front desk, and as soon as O'Malley rounded the corner, Zengo stepped in his way.

"WHA—!" Zengo yelled as he spilled his cup.

"Dang it, Zengo!" O'Malley shouted, looking down to wipe hot chocolate off his shirt for the second day straight. Zengo chuckled.

"Don't worry, O'Malley. Look, cup's empty. I'm just messin' with ya."

O'Malley smiled. "You're lucky, rookie! I'd have had you cleaning the fast food bags outta my car!"

"Yeah, so about the fast food . . ." Zengo poked at O'Malley's gut.

"Don't start," said O'Malley. "I want to show you something. Come here."

O'Malley led them over to his desk and pulled out an envelope. "I stopped by the bank security office on the way in this morning." He showed Zengo six photographs. "These were taken before, during, and after the time shown on Hopkins's ATM receipt."

Zengo bent over the shots. Hopkins was in all of them. He was wearing some sort of sports cap with a bill pulled down so far it hid most of his face, but the green, spot-covered skin was clearly visible on the back of his neck. He was looking over his shoulder in most of the pictures, as though he was afraid of being noticed. "So where are you now, fella?" whispered

Zengo to the frog in the photos.

Sanchez from Forensics approached their desks carrying a file, which he tossed at O'Malley. "Nothing," he said. "No sign of the car that left the tire tracks, nothing turned up on the professor's jacket, and, worse yet, the fish in the duffel—all of it synthetic. I don't know what Hopkins was into, but it wasn't good."

"Looks like we have our work cut out for us then," said O'Malley.

"Pretty fishy situation," said Sanchez. "Good luck." He headed back to Forensics.

"Listen, I think we should check out the high school," said Zengo. "Go through some of the prof's paperwork. Maybe interview a few students and teachers."

"That's a great idea," said O'Malley, standing back up. "My kids will be delighted to see me. Let's hit the road."

"Great, I'll drive." Zengo snatched the keys O'Malley was twirling in his flippers.

"Like heck you will." O'Malley snatched them back.

EAST KALAMAZOO MIDDLE/HIGH SCHOOL, 9:25 A.M.

As the detectives walked up to the main school entrance, Zengo was surprised to see a very long telephoto lens poking out of a hedge just to the left of the door. He reached out to bat it away.

"Heyyyyy! Watch out!" whined a familiar voice. "That thing is expensive!"

"Derek Doherty, is that you?" snapped O'Malley. "Come out of there."

The little reporter stepped around from the back of the hedge, some branches of which were clinging onto his trench coat. He shook them off, then glared at the cops. "You guys again," he said. "What are you doing here?"

"We're auditioning for the glee club. More importantly, what are you doing here?" snapped O'Malley.

"I'm hot on the tracks of this illegal fish story," said Doherty. "There have been rumors of the synthetic stuff making its way through the halls of Kal East for weeks, and now a high school teacher disappears in an illegal deal gone wrong? Something is fishy, if you catch my drift."

"Yeah, we get it," said Zengo. He leaned in closer. "Look, you want the same thing we do: to solve this case. Let's help each other out."

Doherty tilted his head and looked at the detectives with a sly grin. "We'll see," he said. "It depends on what I find out. Sometimes cops end up on the wrong side of right." With a tip of his fedora, he slithered off down the street.

O'Malley rolled his eyes. "That guy sure gets under my fur," he said.

In the front office, the detectives were greeted by the secretary, who was simultaneously writing out tardy slips for students and answering calls from upset parents.

"Please, have a seat. Principal McKeever will be with you shortly."

Zengo pulled up a chair. It was the kind with the desk connected to it.

"I feel like I'm a kid again, in trouble for passing notes," said Zengo.

"So, what? It feels like two weeks ago?"

"Sorry, O'Malley, I forgot, they hadn't invented school yet when you were a kid."

O'Malley ignored him, and pulled up a desk for himself, struggling to squeeze himself into the chair. He inhaled, shook his hips, and shimmied his way in.

"You need help, O'Malley?"

"Stuff it, kid." His belly spilled over the desk. "Just been a while since I've sat in one of these."

The phones rang off the hook. With all of the kids coming in late, it was even busier than PPS headquarters. Everywhere Zengo looked, kids were eating fish with friends. A group of cheerleaders had set up a stand outside the auditorium, selling sushi to raise money for charity. Was any of it legit? Zengo was starting to realize why curbing the illegal fish trade was so big a problem.

"Yes, ma'am," said the secretary, speaking into one of the phones, "we're doing our best at Kal East to stop illegal fish at our front doors. I can assure you that our cafeteria fish have been purchased only from licensed fish dealers. But there's no effective way to test the fish that kids are buying on their own, or to tell where it's coming from."

Finally, her intercom buzzed. Continuing to man all her phones, the secretary waved them toward Principal McKeever's office. Zengo stood up, but

O'Malley didn't budge. He couldn't. He wiggled; he shook. But it was of no use.

Zengo hid a smile and held out his arm. "C'mon, what are partners for?"

O'Malley stretched out his hand to Zengo for help. Zengo grabbed ahold of O'Malley, placed one foot on the chair, and pulled as hard as he could. After a few tugs, O'Malley came stumbling out of the chair. He got up off the floor just as Principal McKeever opened his office door.

"Gentlemen. Please, come on in."

The detectives followed the principal into his brightly lit corner office. Zengo looked out the window at the front courtyard and the football field. Construction workers, all wearing "Pandini

Construction" vests, were running every which way, getting things ready for Friday's big game, the first on the new field.

"Please, take a seat," said the principal. There were two chairs. Both had desks connected to them.

"Thanks, Principal McKeever," said Zengo.

O'Malley, after a moment, sighed and squeezed himself in again.

"So," said Principal McKeever. "I can probably guess why you're here."

"We're here to learn a little bit more about one of your teachers, William Hopkins, who went missing earlier this week," said O'Malley.

"Ah yes, Bill. One of our finest teachers. Such a shame what's happened to him. Is it all true? Our kids have wild imaginations, but the rumors are coming in from so many directions."

"What've you heard?" asked O'Malley.

"That he was involved in an illegal fish deal gone bad. Frankly, gentlemen, I find it hard to believe this to be the case."

"Well, it's true that he's connected to illegal fish in some way," said O'Malley. "How, exactly, we don't know for certain yet. And it's true we can't find him.

You should know, sir, that the preliminary investigation indicates that Professor Hopkins may have been killed."

"I see," said the principal, shaking his head. "A tragedy. Terrible, just terrible."

"A lot of kids out there are buying and selling fish, sir." Zengo nodded toward the hallway.

"We thought, as everyone did, that the illegal fish trade went belly-up with Frank Pandini Sr.'s arrest," said the principal, still shaking his head. "It's been years since the city has had any problems with illegal fish, and we certainly haven't seen it in the high school in years. And then, suddenly, these fish are everywhere. We tell the kids you get what you pay for—but kids are experimenting with fish bought from the back alleys to save a few bucks, and they're getting sick. And for what? To be as cool as the kids whose parents can afford to pack their lunch boxes with top-shelf seafood? Illegal fish was always a concern for our hardworking fisherman, but never an issue of safety. Kids these days don't know their limits or the consequences of their actions. And I find myself wondering, as I'm sure you do, how do we put a stop to this? How do we discern the illegal fish from the legitimate variety?"

"Do you think Hopkins was the middleman here at Kal East?" asked Zengo.

"I'm afraid I don't have any idea. I wish that I had been able to pay closer attention to my old friend. I noticed in passing that he had been acting a little strangely, but given everything going on"—McKeever gestured toward the construction outside—"it's been tough to keep tabs on every teacher in school. There's been a huge push to get the new stadium finished. We have only a few days left before the football season starts. If we make it to the state finals this year, it would mean a lot to our school, not to mention to Mr. Pandini, who has invested so much in our success. Coach Morrissey has put together a stellar team, and the Pirates—er . . . I mean, the Pandas could go all the way this year."

"You think we could take a look at Hopkins's office?" O'Malley asked.

"Why yes, I'd be happy to show you. Please, follow me." Principal McKeever and Zengo stood up. But poor O'Malley was, once again, stuck.

"Sir, you don't have a crowbar, do you?" asked Zengo.

* * *

Principal McKeever ushered the detectives into Hopkins's office. There were stacks of papers strewn across his desk, books spilling out of bookshelves. "It's been untouched since his absence," said Principal McKeever.

As Zengo and O'Malley surveyed the mess, a member of Pandini's construction crew entered the office and whispered something in the principal's ear. "All right," McKeever said, turning to the detectives, "I'll leave you boys to it. Lots of business to attend to. It never stops when you're steering the ship!" He backed out of the room and disappeared.

The detectives found themselves alone amid the professor's clutter.

"I don't know about you," said Zengo, staring at the space where the principal and the construction worker had just stood, "but it seems like a big coincidence that illegal fish have started appearing all over school just as an army of Pandini employees have started working on the grounds."

O'Malley gave him a searching look. "Let's concentrate on Hopkins for now," he finally said.

"Where do we start?" Zengo asked.

"I'll take a look through this filing cabinet. Why don't you check out the papers on his desk?"

Zengo picked up a stack of papers and stepped over another stack on his way to Hopkins's desk chair. "Looks like Teach was a big Kal East Pirates fan," said Zengo, pointing to the pennants and framed articles on the wall over Hopkins's desk. He pulled down a photo of Professor Hopkins at a game. In the picture, a much-younger Hopkins was wearing a Pirates cap and was flanked by star athletes of generations past.

"The hat he's wearing in this picture isn't just retro, it's vintage," said O'Malley, who had come up behind him. "He must have been teaching here a long time, probably started not long after I graduated." He looked at the framed articles going back twenty years. "I just can't understand why he would decide to put his reputation at risk."

"Money?" asked Zengo.

O'Malley looked at him, but just shrugged.

"If you're looking for information on Mr. Hopkins's disappearance, I'd check Blake Cameron's file," said a high-pitched, unfamiliar voice.

Zengo and O'Malley spun around to see a lanky student standing in the doorway.

"And you are . . . ?" asked Zengo.

"Shawn Freeman," he said, not moving. Zengo looked at O'Malley, and could tell he was thinking the same thing Zengo was: this must be the son of the fisherman they had met yesterday. "Professor Hopkins was one of the best teachers in the school. It's not true, what people are saying about him and the illegal fish."

"How do you know that?" asked O'Malley.

"Hopkins was a good man, and he loved the school. I don't believe that he was involved with illegal fish. That's not him."

"And what does Blake Cameron have to do with anything?" asked O'Malley.

"If anyone was going to set up Professor Hopkins as an illegal fish dealer, it was rich-boy Blake Cameron," said Shawn, clicking his claws together. "The professor was just about the only one at this school who didn't worship the quarterback."

The detectives shared a look. Shawn continued, "Everyone knows Blake wasn't passing English. No passing grade, no place on the football team. No place on the football team, no championship for the school. It wasn't a popular decision, but Hopkins did what was right. Blake's a rich kid who only cares about himself. His parents buy him whatever he wants. Money can buy you flashy cars, but it can't buy you a good grade in Professor Hopkins's class. If anyone had a reason to make Hopkins disappear, it was Blake."

Zengo looked to O'Malley. The crustacean was throwing out quite the accusation. "Thanks again for the tip, kid," said O'Malley. "We'll be exploring all possible leads." O'Malley began to shut the door, but Shawn held out his claw.

"If you need to find Blake, you'll probably find him down at the gym." And with that, Shawn finally scuttled backward out of the room. O'Malley shut the door and turned back to Zengo.

"I'm two steps ahead of you, old man," said Zengo, opening up the filing cabinet. "You might want a look in Vanessa's new boyfriend's file anyway, huh?"

O'Malley took the file and went through the assignments, Zengo looking over his shoulder. Paper after paper was covered with red pen. There was no grade above a C-. It was true. This jock-head was not doing well in Hopkins's class.

"Maybe Shawn's on to something," Zengo said. "Nearly flunking, hanging around the docks. . . . This is starting to smell worse than what we found in that wooden crate."

"You think you're suspicious," said O'Malley. "How do you think I feel?" Now he was flipping through Hopkins's appointment book. "Hmm. You'd think someone who got a little help after school might make a bit better grades."

"He never showed up for extra help?" asked Zengo.

"On the contrary," said O'Malley, turning the book around to show Zengo. "He met with Professor Hopkins almost every day for the last few weeks."

"How about if you and I go down to the gym and shoot a few hoops?" suggested Zengo.

EAST KALAMAZOO MIDDLE/HIGH SCHOOL
GYMNASIUM, 10:17 A.M.

The detectives stepped into the gym. It was massive. The sounds of sneakers squeaking against the polished boards filled the room from floor to ceiling. Basketballs bounced, dribbled, and whizzed toward baskets. Zengo spotted the coach in the corner, who carried a clipboard and was dressed head-to-tail in a tracksuit. He nudged O'Malley and pointed.

"Nice work, spotting the coach in a gym full of kids," ribbed O'Malley. "Let's go have a chat." The detectives walked the perimeter of the gym, ducking stray balls along the way.

When they got to the coach, they flashed their badges at the same time. O'Malley took the lead. "Detectives Rick Zengo and Corey O'Malley here. We'd like to have a few words with you."

The coach seemed to hesitate for a moment. Then he blew his whistle. "Kids, keep the games going." He stretched his paw out for a handshake. Zengo took it. It was firm and confident.

"I'm Coach Morrissey. I teach gym and I'm also head coach of the varsity football team. The Fighting Pandas are taking it all the way this year, I guarantee it. What can I do for you guys?"

"We're looking for information on the whereabouts of Professor Hopkins," O'Malley said.

Zengo studied Coach Morrissey's reaction. The coach didn't seem surprised.

"Hmph. Well, sometimes, when you play with fire, you get burned."

"What do you mean?" pressed Zengo.

"Illegal fish," said the coach, shaking his head. "Hopkins was on a downward spiral. Nobody around here would believe he could be mixed up in it, not the upstanding professor. But I heard the guy had money problems. He was probably looking to make a few extra bucks here and there and, well . . . that's what you get. Trouble. Besides, Hopkins wasn't exactly a team player."

"And what do you mean by that?" Zengo took a step closer.

"Well, I mean he wasn't really . . . he didn't care much for the welfare of the students. I'm not saying I wished any harm on the guy. He just, you know, only cared about the numbers. Every kid learns in a different way, and Hopkins wouldn't cut any of my kids a break."

"Your kids?" said O'Malley.

"Yeah, the football players. Morning practices, afternoon practices—it's a busy lifestyle. I'm not saying they should get marks they don't deserve, but . . . a little bit of understanding wouldn't have been out of line. Especially for Blake Cameron."

Zengo and O'Malley exchanged glances, and the coach smiled. "Yeah, I knew that's what this was about. Blake's a good kid. Sure, he wasn't doing well in Hopkins's class, but I promise you he didn't have anything to do with his disappearance." Coach Morrissey looked at his watch. "Excuse me, detectives."

He blew his whistle. It was shrill, and Zengo winced. "Class is over, everyone! Hit the showers and get yourselves to your next class on time, please. I don't want to deal with any more angry teachers barking at me, okay?"

The students dispersed, some sneaking in a few more shots before heading back to the locker rooms.

"We were wondering if we might be able to talk to Blake," Zengo asked.

Coach Morrissey gave the detectives a look.

"Just in the interest of being thorough," O'Malley added.

The coach turned slowly and called out, "Blake, come on over here for a moment, please."

Blake was walking back to the locker room with his classmates, tossing a basketball back and forth. He jogged over, but his pace slowed and his face froze when he saw O'Malley and Zengo.

As he approached the detectives, he swallowed deeply and extended his hand to O'Malley.

"Hello, sir, I'm Blake. I believe you're Vanessa's dad. It's nice to meet you."

O'Malley took his hand and shook.

Zengo looked Blake full in the eyes. "Where were you yesterday morning before eleven a.m.?"

"Zengo . . . ," O'Malley started, in a low voice.

"I saw you yesterday down by the docks," said Zengo, ignoring him. "Right where Hopkins's jacket was found. Criminals always return to the scene of the crime. Don't they, kid?"

Blake began to shake. "I . . . I don't know what you're talking about," he said.

Coach Morrissey stepped in. "Blake was at school yesterday. I had bus duty yesterday morning and I saw him myself. He pulled up in his car, parked in the student lot at eight a.m., right on time."

"And if we double-check the school's security cameras, we'll see that shiny red car of yours remain in the parking lot until the dismissal bell?" Zengo's gaze remained fixed on Blake.

"Sorry, Detective, school's security cameras are in the process of being upgraded."

O'Malley placed his flipper gently on Blake's shoulder. "Kid, listen. Professor Hopkins is missing. Living

113

or dead—we don't know. We know you've been meeting with him a lot lately. Is there anything you can tell us that could help us in this case?"

Blake cleared his throat nervously. At that moment, Vanessa rushed into the gym, her eyes blazing.

"*Dad!*" she said fiercely. "What are you doing?" She marched up to the group, wedging herself in between Blake and her father.

"Calm down, Vanessa," O'Malley said. Zengo was frozen to the spot—this was *not* his department. "We're just asking Blake a couple questions."

"If you're interested in my social life, you can just interrogate me at dinner like usual!" She shot her father a look and grabbed Blake by the arm. "Come on, we're going to be late for class."

Zengo looked back and forth between O'Malley and the retreating back of his daughter, unsure of what to say. So far, these inquiries weren't going too well, he thought. He glanced at O'Malley for the next move.

"We've got a few more questions for you and your team," said O'Malley. "I wonder if we could continue this after school?"

"The offensive line has a training session this afternoon at Roar," said the coach.

"Roar, eh?" said Zengo. "What a coincidence."

O'Malley smacked the back of Zengo's knees with his tail. "We'll catch you there, then," he said.

"Suit yourself," said the coach. "Not sure any of us have much to tell you." He headed out of the gym.

"What a tool," said Zengo, rubbing the back of his knees. "What happened with your daughter back there? Do you always let your kids walk away with the prime suspect in a murder case?"

O'Malley shot him a look. "It's not a murder case—yet. And Blake's not a suspect. But I can't shake the feeling he knows something."

"That makes two of us. And this is the second time in as many days that we're following a lead to a Pandini establishment, I couldn't help but notice." Zengo picked up a stray basketball and took a shot.

Swish! Nothing but net.

ROAR, 4:10 P.M.

On the way to Roar, Zengo made what was possibly his worst tactical error of the day. When O'Malley suggested they step into Frank's Franks for a couple of triple chili chow dogs, Zengo refused to get one. "I don't want to give that panda one penny," he said stubbornly.

"Suit yourself," said O'Malley, wolfing down his first dog before they even got back to the car. He finished the second dog before they got to Roar, and tossed the bag full of extra ketchup and mustard onto the floor by Zengo's feet. "Rule number one," O'Malley said, "keep a clean car." He smiled. "I'll admit, I'm not very good at that rule."

Zengo kicked the bag under the seat and hoped O'Malley didn't hear the rumbling of his stomach.

They drove up to Roar and found a parking spot on the adjacent street. O'Malley parallel parked and turned off the ignition. Parked right in front of them was a brand-new Range Rover with a GOPANDAS license plate.

"Tsk, tsk," said O'Malley. "I think I spot a parking violation."

"Why are you bothering with parking violations at a time like this?" said Zengo. "That's not even our job. Let a meter maid take care of it."

"Want to run that plate for me while I write the ticket?" asked O'Malley.

Zengo was still confused, but he took the squad car's laptop and punched in the plate number. Coach Morrissey's license photo flashed on the screen, seemingly sneering at Zengo for even looking. Zengo wondered if O'Malley already knew that the ride was registered to the fox.

He also wondered how a high school football coach could afford a brand-new Range Rover. Coach Morrissey's ride was baller status—just not the level of game that Morrissey dealt with. Zengo got out, walked over to the coach's car, crouched down, and inspected the sparkling rims. He stood up and peered inside for a closer look at the pristine leather interior. "Wow! Next year's model! You need to know people who know people to get ahold of a set of wheels like this. You also need buckets of cash."

O'Malley tapped Zengo on the arm. "Well, looks like Morrissey knows people who know people." He pointed to the second-floor window of Roar. There, Zengo saw Coach Morrissey schmoozing it up with a shadowy figure with broad shoulders and a white tuxedo. There was no mistaking who it was.

Zengo saw Pandini place his hand on Morrissey's shoulder. The two laughed and clinked glasses.

"I'd like to know what in the what is so dang funny about a missing professor and a city that's besieged by illegal fish," O'Malley grumbled.

"Well, maybe we should charge in there and ask!" Zengo pulled out his badge and motioned for the door.

"Hold on, cowboy. I have a plan. Let's get back in the car and wait for practice to be over."

Zengo's adrenaline was surging, but he saw something in his partner's eye he hadn't seen before.

"Trust me," said O'Malley.

They got back into the squad car. O'Malley leaned his seat back and put the newspaper over his face. "I'm going to catch a little beauty sleep for a few minutes, rookie," he said. "You keep an eye on things."

Zengo couldn't believe it. They were on a stakeout, and his partner was *snoozing*? Once again, it was all up to him. He checked the grip on his boomerang, determined that at least *one* of them be on alert.

Ten minutes later, Morrissey walked out of the gym. He pulled the bright orange slip off his windshield, clearly not pleased to find a parking ticket on his car. "Aw, man! Not again."

Zengo turned to wake O'Malley, but he was already up and alert and opening the door of the car.

"Watch and learn," said O'Malley. He exited and stepped up to Morrissey. Zengo slunk low in his seat and rolled down the window so he could hear.

"Bummer, Morrissey," said O'Malley, taking off his sunglasses. "Nice set of wheels you got here. Bet some meter maid was just jealous." He took the ticket from the coach. "Don't worry about this. I'll get this back to the station, make sure it's taken care of." He stuffed the ticket into his breast pocket. "Don't give it a second thought."

"Really? Oh wow, thanks!" Morrissey relaxed his shoulders.

"You just focus on giving us a winning team. We all want to see the Pirates—I mean, the Pandas—take home the championship. Speaking of which, it's pretty sweet that the offensive line gets to come down here to train." O'Malley nodded to Roar. "I used to throw around the football for Kal East back in my day. We would've killed for a facility like this."

Morrissey leaned against his car. "Yeah, I've been bringing some of the guys down here to work out. Pandini himself gave us free memberships."

"Wow! What a guy. He sure is doing a lot for the athletic department. This city could use more philanthropists like good ol' Frank."

"Ain't that the truth," said the coach. "Pandini's a real class act. All he asks for is a championship banner."

"Is that right?"

"Well, it's the least we could do to thank him. He deserves nothing less. That's why I have the guys working so hard. I bring my kids down here to pump some iron. We've got a killer team this year."

"Thanks to Blake," said O'Malley.

The coach considered O'Malley for a moment. "You know, Blake's a bright kid. English isn't his strong suit, but he's a good kid, and a hard worker."

"That's not what I heard."

"And who told you otherwise?"

"One of Blake's classmates, Shawn Freeman."

Morrissey sneered. "Freeman has had it out for Blake since day one. Just because Blake's family is rich and Shawn's dad is a dockworker doesn't mean that Blake is some sort of villain. It didn't help when Shawn unsuccessfully tried out for the JV football squad. We made him the team mascot—we try to be as inclusive as possible at Kal East. But still, Shawn continues to direct his animosity to Blake and the other guys on the team. The only time he's supportive is when he's suited up and working the crowd."

O'Malley smiled. "I know how it is. Everyone's jealous of the ballplayers. They always end up with the pretty girls. And with the nice cars, too." O'Malley looked up and down at Morrissey's sparkling Range Rover.

"Yeah, she is a beauty! It's on loan from Pandini while my car is in the shop. That guy is committed to the teachers in this town, if you know what I mean." Morrissey smiled—a little uncomfortably, Zengo thought—as O'Malley admired his wheels.

Just then, Blake stepped out of Roar, a towel around his neck and clearly exhausted after an intense workout. He approached O'Malley and offered yet another handshake. "Hello, sir. I'm really sorry for everything back there at school."

"No sweat," said O'Malley.

The rest of the offensive line came barreling out of the gym. A bunch of knuckleheads, thought Zengo. Typical jocks.

"Well, if you'll excuse us, Detective, I need to get these kids back to school to catch their rides," said Coach Morrissey. "They've got homework to tend to. Right, boys?"

"Yes, Coach, sir!" they said in unison.

Most of the kids threw their duffel bags into the trunk and piled into the Rover, but Blake stepped aside. "Thanks, Coach, but I think I'm just going to walk over to my dad's office. He works a few blocks from here and he's pulling another late night. He'll bring me by the school to pick up my car."

"Suit yourself, Blake. Make sure you study hard for that history quiz you have on Friday!"

O'Malley got back into the car. As Morrissey peeled around the corner and Blake sauntered away, Zengo said, "Did you catch a good look at their duffel bags?"

"Yup. Same as the one we found down on the docks."

"Another coincidence, huh?" said Zengo.

O'Malley smiled at him and started the engine. "A few too many, I think."

"And why would Morrissey tell you the Rover is on loan when it's registered in his name?"

"Why do you think, rook? He's trying to hide something. What, exactly, we've yet to uncover." O'Malley put the car in drive and pulled away from the curb.

Zengo grinned as his stomach rumbled again. *Note to self*, he thought. *Don't skip lunch, even if O'Malley will only stop at the greasiest hot dog stand in town.* As O'Malley was distracted by the afternoon traffic, Zengo stealthily picked up one of the leftover packets of ketchup. Turning his face to the window, he bit into it and sucked it dry, hoping O'Malley didn't notice.

PLATYPUS POLICE SQUAD HEADQUARTERS, 6:00 P.M.

Sergeant Plazinski paced in front of his office window, his figure framed by the city skyline. "So this Blake kid, does he have a criminal record?"

"None, sir," said Zengo. "I hate to say it, but he's clean. I can't say I trust him, and I know I saw him down at the docks, but we can't find any other blemish on the kid's transcript, or any reason to keep investigating him for now. Though O'Malley wants to keep some surveillance on him. After all, Blake *is* dating his daughter." Zengo smirked and took a sip of his hot chocolate.

O'Malley opened his bill to say something, but Plazinski shushed him and resumed pacing. "His choice in girlfriends aside, I think you detectives are right. Blake is likely a dead end. If Blake is so committed to the football team, he wouldn't put himself at risk, going after a teacher or getting mixed up in illegal fish."

"That still leaves Coach Morrissey, though," said O'Malley. "He's got a stake in Blake staying on the team at all costs, and he's got no love for Hopkins. Plus his stories aren't adding up."

"And if we're making a list of the people who are anxious to keep Blake Cameron in a uniform," said Zengo, "I think Pandini should be right at the top. OW!" Zengo yelped as O'Malley stomped on his foot.

"What are you talking about?" said Plazinski, who abruptly ceased pacing to look from Zengo to O'Malley. He appeared puzzled and, Zengo realized, a little angry. He didn't care.

"Come on, isn't it obvious?" Zengo said. "Frank Pandini! The gym bags from Roar match the bag that was filled with the fish, and Pandini has poured a ton of money into making a team that can go all the way this year. Without Blake, the season is shot, and with

Hopkins in the picture, Blake wasn't going to be able to play. Look, I know none of this evidence is conclusive, but it's suspicious is all I'm saying."

Plazinski sat on his desk and looked at both detectives. He turned to O'Malley. "What do you think?"

O'Malley was quiet for a few moments. "The kid does have a point, sir," O'Malley finally said, carefully. "There's nothing here that we can pin on Pandini, but it's worth exploring a little bit more."

"You're right," Plazinski said, and Zengo finally felt some relief. But only for a moment. "There isn't nearly enough evidence," the sergeant continued. "That is why you are to stay clear of Pandini. He isn't the only one who benefits from a winning team. And duffel bags from Roar come free with every new membership to the club."

"But Sarge, Pandini—"

Plazinski cut Zengo off cold. "But nothing. The answer is no. It's a dangerous road to go down without solid, concrete evidence. I'm not going to risk the reputation of the PPS or the goodwill of Mr. Pandini by investigating him on a hunch. The mayor would roast me if we're wrong, and it's a waste of resources on top of it."

"Sir, with all due respect, things are definitely not what they seem in Pandini's empire. And if you scratch the surface a bit, I don't think this ends with Hopkins. Are we supposed to think it's a coincidence that illegal fish showed up in schools right when Pandini's construction goons started building the new stadium?" O'Malley was grinding his heel into Zengo's foot by now and Zengo saw the veins on Plazinski's forehead start to rise, but he couldn't contain himself.

"Rookie, why would a guy like Pandini, who has made millions in real estate dealings, risk it all for a little action from illegal fish? He's worked hard to build his name in this city, and I hardly can imagine he would squander all of his hard work with seedy activities down by the docks. I don't need to remind you that everything we've got here at headquarters comes courtesy of Pandini's generosity, including the seats you're sitting in!" Zengo and O'Malley shifted in their chairs. *They're not even comfortable*, Zengo thought.

"Well, before he could erect that first skyscraper, he had to make his first dollar somewhere—"

Zengo was silenced by the sound of Plazinski pounding on his desk.

"You are not to pursue this! What part of that don't you understand?" He stared hard at Zengo for a moment before standing up straight again. This was not the sergeant Zengo had met just yesterday. "Now listen up, and listen good: the key to this whole case is the same as it was yesterday. We need to find Hopkins. Our divers didn't find anything in their sweep of the bay, and this is starting to look less like a murder and more like a missing-person case. Either Hopkins is on the lam, or he was kidnapped. If we want to get to the bottom of this, we need to locate him. Your only priority is to do just that. That's *it*. Now get out of my office."

O'Malley dragged Zengo out of Plazinski's eyesight before the sarge started throwing things. Plazinski slammed the door behind them.

"You don't want to be in a room with Plazinski when he gets that angry. Heck, you don't want to be in the same zip code," whispered O'Malley.

As if things couldn't get worse, a snickering Diaz and Lucinni were waiting for them. They had heard everything.

"Pandini, really?" said Diaz. "Rookie, who's next? Should we haul the president in for questioning?"

"Did the queen of England drive the getaway car?"

"And hey, hasn't the Tooth Fairy been acting awfully suspicious lately?"

"Diaz and Lucinni represent!" said Lucinni, and they high-fived.

Peggy came by with her mail cart. "Detectives . . . Diaz . . . and . . . Lucinni. More . . . reports . . . have come . . . in . . . on . . . illegal—"

"Yeah, yeah, yeah, Peggy. Illegal fish, we got it. Just leave the messages on our desk with the other ones. Hey, Diaz, let's go get some coffee." The jokers' laughter trailed off as they walked down the hall. Peggy shrugged and pushed her cart away as Zengo stomped back to his desk.

O'Malley fired up

his computer. Zengo, clicking a pen anxiously, didn't know what to do with himself. He stopped abruptly and looked to O'Malley for some kind of reaction, but nothing. Finally, he blurted out, "Why didn't you stand up for me back there?"

O'Malley glanced up from his screen. "Okay, rook, I agree that everything with Pandini is looking mighty fishy. But at the end of the day, the sarge is right. There isn't enough to make a move on him."

Zengo crossed his brows. "That's when cases go unsolved. When cops are too timid to make a move."

O'Malley sat back in his chair. "Listen, kid, we're not going to get anywhere forcing the Pandini angle. I know it's your instinct to follow your hunch, but trust me, you need to set it aside here."

"And you need to pay attention to your instincts, if you even have any left."

O'Malley didn't give Zengo the satisfaction of a reaction. He turned back to his computer and continued typing. Zengo leaned on his desk with his head in his hands. He almost jumped when O'Malley's phone rang. Zengo reached for it himself, thinking it could be a hot tip, but O'Malley glanced at him, then let it ring once more before he picked it up.

"Hello? Oh, hi, dear. No—I mean, no. Of course I'm going to come home tonight. It's just that—yes, you have given me four wonderful children—yes, I appreciate everything you do. Dinner? What? No, I'm sure he has plans. No. Honey. Really? Ugh! Fine. Okay. I'll ask him. I will! I promise." He hung up and looked at his partner.

"What's up?" asked Zengo.

"My wife has invited you over for dinner."

Zengo and O'Malley stared at each other for a moment, neither one making a move.

"Well," said Zengo slowly, "I suppose we shouldn't keep her waiting."

"No," O'Malley said without emotion. "We shouldn't."

THE O'MALLEY HOUSEHOLD, 7:00 P.M.

As they pulled up at the O'Malley home again, Zengo couldn't help thinking about how it compared to his family's spacious home on the other side of town. The O'Malleys' house looked neat and solid from the outside. But it was small—especially for a family the size of O'Malley's.

Just like in a TV show, O'Malley opened the front door and called, "Honey, I'm home!" He led Zengo past the threshold of the entryway, stepping over book bags along the way.

Declan and Jonathan bolted to the front door. "Hey,

Dad!" they called out. O'Malley smiled and opened his arms for a hug. But they ran past his outstretched arms and straight to Zengo, offering him high fives, which he returned.

O'Malley stepped over the boys' socks and underwear, spilling out of the laundry room. "Karen!" he shouted as he picked up a baby, who was crawling underfoot. "Come meet my new partner."

"Oh, hi, dear." Karen turned the corner. Zengo could tell she had dressed up for the occasion, and he could tell that O'Malley noticed. He was touched, and a little embarrassed.

"Hi. I'm Detective Rick Zengo—but please, call me Rick!" Zengo took her flipper and, on an impulse, kissed it. "A pleasure, Mrs. O'Malley."

Smoke billowed from the kitchen. "Oh, crud!" she yelled, and dashed off to battle the blaze. "It's so nice to meet you!" she shouted. "Sit down; dinner will be right on the table. And call me Karen! Corey, can you take care of Lissy?"

O'Malley arched his brows as he buckled the baby into her high chair.

"So what's it like to be a detective?" Jonathan asked after they'd all sat down to eat.

O'Malley put down his fork with a clatter. "You know, Johnny, there's someone you see every day who's also a detective."

Jonathan ignored his dad and even ignored being called Johnny. He looked over at Zengo, who hid a smile behind his flipper. Well, after two days, he had an answer, Zengo guessed. "It's pretty cool. You get to drive real fast, you get to have a boomerang, you get to wear cool sunglasses. And you get to take down the bad guys!"

"That's so awesome!"

"Honey, would you please pass me the casserole?" O'Malley asked, clearly a little perturbed. Zengo guessed Jonathan hadn't ever asked his dad about being a detective.

"It's right next to you, sweetie," said Karen, turning back to Zengo. "So, Rick, tell me—did you always want to be a detective?"

"Sort of," said Zengo. "I've always liked helping people. And I feel like I've been pretty lucky in my life, so, when I grew up, I thought I'd just try to help other people. Keep them safe, make the city as nice a place to live as I could."

"Corey here always wanted to be a cop, too. Isn't

that right, dear?" Karen patted her husband on the knee. She turned to Zengo. "Did he tell you all about his early days on the beat?"

O'Malley nearly choked on his milk. "Karen, honey, he doesn't want to hear about any of that. . . ."

Zengo perked up. "Early days?"

"You never told him about the time you took out six baddies with one boomerang throw?" said Karen.

"Oh, that was nothing," said O'Malley, blushing.

"What about the time you single-handedly solved that string of robberies at the rubber works?" said Karen.

"That was a good day," agreed O'Malley. "But it wasn't just me; the whole squad—"

"And I'm sure he told you all about the days when Frank Pandini Sr. ran the city," said Karen. "If it weren't for my dear Corey-bear here, Pandini might have never been brought into custody."

"Wow, I had no idea," said Zengo. He looked over at O'Malley, who seemed to have gotten very interested in pushing one piece of casserole around on his plate.

"You're working with a genuine hero, Rick," said Karen. "Corey was handpicked by his boss, Lieutenant Dailey, to be part of—"

Zengo leaned forward at the mention of his grandpa's name, but O'Malley cleared his throat and turned to his kids, evidently to change the subject. "So, kids, how was school today?"

"Everyone is all sorts of stressed out because of the big game." Vanessa spoke for the first time that evening. "Cheerleaders can be so tightly wound when they want their cheers to be just perfect. And with the new mascot and all, they have to come up with all new rhymes. We're finally getting a chance to try everything out in front of people at the pep rally tonight, but if there are any problems, we won't have much time to fix them before Friday. And I really want everything to be perfect for Blake's big game!"

Zengo shot O'Malley a look. *Everyone sure is concerned about Blake and his big game*, he thought.

Vanessa's phone beeped. She snapped it up and opened a text.

"Vanessa, what did we say about gizmos at the dinner table?" said O'Malley.

"Sorry, Dad. I'm working out a ride to the pep rally tonight."

"Where? When? And with whom?" asked O'Malley.

Three of the five *W*s, Zengo noticed. Must be rough

having a detective for a father.

"Bamboo, eight p.m., Blake and Phoebe," she answered. Clearly she was familiar with the drill.

"Sweetie, I don't know. That's all the way on the other side of town. It's a school night." Zengo knew what O'Malley was worried about, even if he wasn't saying it outright: Bamboo made him nervous.

"But Dad . . ."

"Vanessa, no buts, please. I'm not so sure about Bamboo. It's expensive, for one thing."

"Dad, all the kids go there! And we have to practice our routine for the game on Friday!"

"I've made my decision, and that's final. You must have homework to do, quizzes to study for. Sorry, the answer is 'negative.'"

"UGH! You just don't understand!" Vanessa stood up from the table, marched upstairs to her room, and slammed the door. At that very moment, Baby Lissy threw her bowl in the air, splattering the brown mush across O'Malley's bill.

Karen glanced at O'Malley with a questioning look on her face. Zengo thought for a moment, and then got up from his chair. "Do you mind if I talk to her?"

"I think that would be fine, Rick." Karen frowned

at O'Malley, who was wiping his face. Jonathan and Declan got up from the table with their plates as Zengo rose and made his way to the stairs.

Zengo knocked on the first door down the hallway. He figured the door plastered with photos of boy bands and magazine-headline collages belonged to neither Declan nor Jonathan.

"What?" Vanessa called from inside.

"Um . . . It's me, Rick."

He heard movement. "Come in."

Zengo cracked the door open and gave a little wave. He stood awkwardly for a moment before speaking. There was more pink and purple in here than he knew

what to do with. He cleared his throat. "It's tough living with your parents, isn't it?"

"Yeah. Especially when you've got a dad who just doesn't get it."

"I live with my parents too," Zengo said. "I love them and everything, but sometimes I wish they'd just leave me alone."

"Tell me about it," Vanessa said. "Every time I want to do something, I get this interrogation. None of my friends have a cop for a dad. All their parents have normal jobs, and decent cars for them to drive around in every once in a while. Dad's still driving around the same clunker from before I was born. It's humiliating." She looked at him. "You probably don't understand what I mean. You're not from this part of town, are you? I can tell, just by the way you dress."

Zengo looked down at his leather jacket, a little embarrassed. "Well, no, I'm not. But my mom grew up right around here, and her dad, my grandpa, was a detective with the PPS. That's why I'm on the squad now. I really looked up to him. I want to be just like him."

"You do?" said Vanessa. "Why?"

"Because he was a real hero," said Zengo. "And so is your dad. He really cares about this city, about

144

keeping it safe. And he cares about you and your family like you wouldn't believe. People like your dad are a big reason why Kalamazoo City is such a great place to live."

Vanessa still looked skeptical. "You wouldn't feel like that if he was your dad," she said.

"Maybe not. But I'm going to have to ask you to trust me on this." Zengo looked back over his shoulder at the door. "Hey, I've got an idea. I bet your dad would feel better about you going to Bamboo if he and I came with you."

"A pep rally with my dad? Are you kidding?" Vanessa began.

"I know, I know," Zengo said. "But it's better to go with him along than not go at all, isn't it? And I promise I'll keep him out of your way. You won't even know that he's there. And more importantly: your friends won't know that he's there. Is it a deal?"

She didn't say anything for a moment. Then she shrugged and said, "Sure. Okay. Whatever."

"Great. And do me a favor," said Zengo, as they headed for the door. "Cut the guy some slack, will you?"

She wrinkled her bill. "I'll think about it."

When they got back to the dining room, O'Malley was just clearing the table while Karen was cleaning up the baby.

"O'Malley," Zengo started, "Vanessa and I were talking, and came up with a plan for the pep rally tonight. One that guarantees she'll be safe at this shindig."

O'Malley looked at him skeptically.

"You and I will accompany her to cheer on the Kal East Pandas as well."

Zengo gave Vanessa a wink to let her know it would be all right. She rolled her eyes in response. It was probably just a reflex.

"Zengo, come over here," said O'Malley. He pulled his partner into the kitchen, and opened his bill to speak, but Zengo started in first.

"Look, O'Malley, you can't make her cancel her plans at the last minute just because the party is at Pandini's place. Besides, it'll give you and me a chance to do some off-duty bonding."

"Oh 'off-duty'? This has nothing to do with sniffing around Pandini's business? Don't you remember what the sarge said?"

"We can't help it if you have to be there to look after

your daughter, now can we?"

Vanessa popped her head around the doorway. "Daddy, please?"

Zengo playfully punched his partner's shoulder. "C'mon, root beer floats are on me!"

"Okay, fine," O'Malley finally consented. "But we're only staying for an hour. It *is* a school night, Vanessa. Did I mention that?"

She jumped over and gave him a peck on the cheek, and disappeared around the corner and back up the stairs to her room. Zengo saw the barest hint of a smile on O'Malley's face.

BAMBOO, 8:10 P.M.

The scene at Bamboo was wild. Roxie belted the school's song into the microphone, the band was in full swing, and hundreds of teenagers filled the spacious dance floor. A banner above the stage read, GO PANDAS!

Zengo and O'Malley sipped root beer floats at a corner table. Zengo had promised O'Malley on the way over he wouldn't go crazy with the interrogations tonight. But Zengo couldn't help but notice that even O'Malley was scanning the crowd, the entryway, behind the bar, and the balcony area a bit more than he might have been usually. If Pandini's crew did have anything to do with selling illegal fish to schoolkids, this would be a prime opportunity for a little extra-curricular activity.

The song ended, and Roxie gave the crowd a wave. Coach Morrissey took the microphone.

"How are my Pandas doin' TONIGHT?" he shouted. The crowd went nuts. Zengo had never seen such excitement at a Kal East pep rally.

Coach Morrissey called the entire team up onstage. The motley crew of athletes barely fit. Mike Lewis, the team's star running back, teetered on the edge of the stage, holding on to the defensive linemen when he nearly lost his balance.

"And let's all hear it for our quarterback, who will be leading us to victory on Friday, Blake Cameron!" The crowd roared even louder. Everyone chanted, "Speech! Speech! Speech!" and Morrissey handed the mic over to Blake, who reluctantly took it.

"Let's hear it for Coach Morrissey!" More cheers filled the room, then fell silent as Blake continued. "No one person is responsible for leading us to victory—Friday night will be about the team. But if there is one person who is most responsible for a win, it's someone who isn't on this stage right now. Tonight has been super cool, and none of this—not the pep rally tonight, not our new uniforms, and especially not the new stadium—would have been possible without the generosity of Mr. Pandini." The crowd erupted once again.

Across the room, Zengo saw Shawn Freeman in his mascot costume, holding the head under one arm. He saw the detectives, too, and came over. "Cheering on the team?" he said with a sneer.

"We've got spirit, yes we do. We've got spirit. . . ." Zengo paused to take a sip of his root beer float. "How

about you? You are the mascot, after all."

"I like the team okay," said Shawn. "It's that lousy phony Blake I can't stand. Rich kids like him have no idea what it's like for the rest of us. My dad is about to lose his job, but as long as the football team has new uniforms, everyone's happy."

The cheerleading squad, led by Vanessa, was getting ready to do its routine.

"Aren't you supposed to be up there?" said Zengo, getting sick of the sight of Shawn Freeman and his dour outlook.

"Yeah," said the mascot, putting his head on. He made his way through the crowd.

"I'm going to get up a little closer to the stage," said O'Malley. "I want to watch my little girl bust some moves."

Zengo remembered his promise to Vanessa. "Do your best to stay out of sight. Don't want to distract her."

"She won't even know I'm nearby. Stealth is my middle name."

Somehow, Zengo doubted that, but he used the opportunity to make a quick scan of the crowded club on his own. He walked around the balcony. He checked behind the bar (and got a couple dirty looks from Carpy). He took a peek in the bathroom. Nothing shady, at least as far as he could tell. He got back to his table as the music was starting for the cheerleading squad.

And then, just past the waving Kal East pennants, beyond the mob of ecstatic teenagers, in the glare of the strobe lights, he saw, by the back door, a flash of black and red that could not be mistaken. A Kal East cap. But not just any Kal East cap—a vintage Kal East cap, pirate and all. Zengo hadn't seen one of those since he was in Hopkins's office. In fact, the person wearing it looked an awful lot like Hopkins. . . .

Zengo bolted up, grabbed his radio, and darted toward the back, wading through the sea of hyped-up high schoolers. The dude in the Pirates cap had slipped into the kitchen and opened the back door and disappeared into the night.

"O'Malley; come in, O'Malley!" Zengo shouted into his radio, but there was no response. Probably couldn't hear him over the noise in the club. But there was no time to waste.

Zengo banged open the back door and spilled out into the alleyway. The night was still, quiet except for the thumping from the club. Zengo was panting heavily, his lungs filled with crisp air. He spun around, looked left, looked right—but there was no sign of the person he'd seen. He ran toward the street and looked both ways. Nothing.

But before he could consider his next move, he heard the back door open again. It was Joey, the Bamboo busboy. Zengo took a few steps back to get a better look, concealing himself behind a trash can. Joey walked into the glow of a streetlamp, and that was when Zengo saw what he was carrying. A duffel bag. A duffel bag with that menacing Roar logo. A duffel bag stuffed with something that looked awfully familiar.

"STOP! PLATYPUS POLICE SQUAD!" Zengo shouted. Joey dropped the duffel and bolted back through the door, Zengo in hot pursuit. The chase blasted through the kitchen. Joey threw frying pans off counters, Zengo dodging each one.

"O'Malley! Come in!" Zengo shouted into his walkie-talkie. "It's that busboy, Joey! I think he was

about to make a deal for illegal fish! He just ran into the club. I'm in hot pursuit."

A crackle in response. O'Malley had finally heard him. "Copy, Zengo! There are only a few ways out of the club, so we need to cut them off. He can't get out of here if he doesn't have an exit. Back off and cover the door you chased him in. I'll cover the front door. This could get ugly, if we chase him into the crowd. Do you copy, rookie?"

"Negative." Zengo heard him, but he wasn't about to let Joey disappear now. He ignored his partner and placed his radio back on his belt.

Joey dodged around a cook and through the door of the kitchen, right into the middle of the dance floor. The cheerleading squad was getting into position to form a pyramid as the bass of the music sped up to a breakneck tempo. Joey pushed his way through teenagers, and seemed to be making his way toward the stairs that led up to the balcony. Was there a roof exit? There wasn't any time to question.

"Halt! Platypus Police Squad!" Zengo shouted. The music abruptly stopped as Zengo pulled out his boomerang. Cheers gave way to shrieks as the kids on the dance floor scattered and the football team hit the deck. Vanessa, nearly at the top of the pyramid, tumbled to the floor as the girls below bailed for safety. Joey looked back over his shoulder, and picked up speed. This was Zengo's one chance. He couldn't let Joey out of his sight. He pulled back and threw the boomerang, aiming right at Joey's legs.

Clean shot! Joey fell face-first onto the dance floor.

By the time O'Malley found them, Zengo was on top of Joey, slapping handcuffs on his wrists.

"You have the right to remain silent," Zengo began as he pulled Joey to his feet.

O'Malley was speechless. He gave Zengo a hard look. *Probably just jealous*, thought Zengo.

A camera flashed. "This'll look great on tomorrow's front page!" said Derek Doherty as he snapped away. Zengo dismissed O'Malley's disapproving glare and posed with Joey, like a fisherman who had just reeled in his first big catch.

CHAPTER 15

PLATYPUS POLICE SQUAD HEADQUARTERS, 9:30 P.M.

Joey sat motionless in the dark interrogation room. There were three chairs—one for him and two for the detectives who had hauled him in. A bare lightbulb dangled over a plain, empty table. Zengo leaned over and breathed within inches of Joey's snout, which was crusted with blood from the fall.

"I'm going to ask you one more time: What were you doing with illegal fish at a school event?"

Joey glared back vacantly and smirked. "I told you . . . I don't know what you're talkin' about. I've got nothing to do with no illegal fish."

161

"Right after we nabbed you, the forensics guys collected the bag you were carrying. We've got the evidence, Joey. Now: start talking."

"I ain't got nothing to say to you two monotremes," he sneered.

This had been going on for an hour already. Zengo was ready to leap across the table when the door flung open. A short but imposing figure in a brown three-piece tailored suit barged in and slammed his briefcase down on the table. "Joey, don't say another word."

Zengo closed his eyes and sighed. He recognized the bird from his billboards.

"Attorney Doug Raskin," the lawyer continued. "And you are rookie detective Rick Zengo, if I'm not mistaken?"

"I've been on the force long enough to know a

criminal when I see one," Zengo snapped.

"But not long enough to know that my client can't be held without evidence or charge any longer than he already has. I look forward to hanging your badge on my wall alongside the other game I've tracked down." Raskin flashed a greasy smile.

O'Malley tried to step in, but Zengo held him back. "Oh, we've got the evidence, big shot. Boys are bringing it in now."

Before anyone could say another word, the door banged open and Plazinski charged in. The sergeant flipped on the overhead fluorescents, flooding the once-ominous room with garish light. His expression sent Zengo's stomach into somersaults. But Zengo had evidence this time. He smiled at Raskin and turned to his boss. "Sarge, I'm glad you're here. Our friend Joey was caught with a duffel full of illegal fish at a pep rally for the high school football team!"

"It ain't true," Joey shouted as he stood up.

"Not another word, rookie," Plazinski said to Zengo.

Raskin patted Joey on the shoulder, guiding him back down to his chair. The battered marsupial sat there, silent, his arms crossed, a smug look on his face.

"The boys are bringing the duffel bag now."

Sanchez walked in with a member of his forensics team. They placed the bag on the table and unzipped it. Before they could do anything else, Zengo thrust his hand into the bag and dramatically pulled out . . . a mouth guard.

Zengo threw it aside and turned the bag upside down. The contents spilled out: boxing gloves, talcum powder, a few towels, and headgear.

Joey laughed and Raskin scoffed as Zengo's heart sank. He looked at O'Malley, who just stared at the floor and shook his head, cupping his forehead with his flippers.

"But I swear! This must not be the same duffel he had then! Somebody tampered with the evidence! This isn't—"

Plazinski cut him off. "I've heard enough, rookie."

"As have I," said Raskin. "Joey, get up, we're leaving." He pulled Joey to his feet.

"Please accept my deepest apologies for any inconvenience this has caused you," said Plazinski as he opened the door for them. "I assure you these detectives will be punished accordingly."

Joey winked at Zengo as he passed. Zengo balled his flippers into fists. But there was nothing he could do.

Once they were gone and Plazinski was alone with his detectives, he exploded.

"My office. NOW!"

Zengo and O'Malley followed the sarge across the floor. As they approached Plazinski's office, they passed Diaz and Lucinni, who gleefully held front-row seats to the theatrics unfolding. The two of them mouthed, "High five!" and slapped webbed hands as Plazinski slammed his office door nearly off its hinges.

Zengo cringed as soon as he and O'Malley were seated in the uncomfortable orange plastic chairs in

Plazinski's office, prepared for the worst. But before the sergeant could open his bill, there was a knock at the door. A hulking silhouette filled the frosted glass. Zengo gulped. O'Malley seemed to be holding his breath. Plazinski blinked.

"Come in," the sergeant called. The door slowly opened. A giant black furry foot stepped in, followed by the massive form of Frank Pandini Jr.

"Gentlemen," he greeted them. "Sergeant, Mr. Raskin has filled me in on the little mix-up from earlier this evening. Would you mind if I had a word with your detectives?"

"Not at all, sir." Plazinski stood up. "Here, please, take my seat. I'll get you a cup of coffee."

Plazinski left, and Pandini came around in front of Zengo and O'Malley. His bulky frame loomed large behind the desk as he stared at the two detectives. There was a moment of silence before he turned to O'Malley.

"Detective Corey O'Malley, is it?"

O'Malley nodded his head.

"You've been on the force awhile, haven't you? You have a long history; you've done a lot of great things for this town." Pandini fiddled with the ring on his

pinky finger. He turned to the rookie detective. "And you, the newest detective on the squad. Zongo, is it?"

Zengo squinted his eyes. His voice was flat. "It's Zengo."

"Zengo, right." Pandini leaned back in the chair. "My apologies. You're lucky, to be partnered with an experienced vet like O'Malley here. Detectives, I want to first tell you I understand that the two of you are doing your jobs. You're out there every day, risking your lives to keep this city safe, and I can't tell you enough how much respect I have for what you do. I am not proud of the things my father did, but I am thankful that there are police officers and detectives who believe in this city, as I do. And as I think I have proven, I am one hundred percent committed to working with the Platypus Police Squad to continue to improve this city and restore glory to the streets my father once filled with fear and greed."

Plazinski returned with the coffee and set it down in front of Pandini, but Pandini didn't even glance at it. He continued. "We have a lot in common, you all and I. We love this city. We want to make it a better place. But here's the difference: I do things. I make progress. I spend my money to build, to create, to construct. You police officers, you are here to prevent. And when you come into my businesses and start throwing around your boomerangs, not to mention false accusations about my employees, you are preventing progress. You are getting in the way. And I'm not about to let a couple loose cannons destroy everything I'm trying so hard to build." He took a sip of the coffee, then surreptitiously spit it back into the cup, grimacing. Plazinski squirmed.

"But I'm not here to make threats. I'll say this once

more: I keep an eye on every employee at all of my businesses. If you have a suspicion, please pay me a visit, and I'm sure we can take care of it without boomerangs and embarrassing mistakes. I'm working toward progress and I do hope that you fine officers of the law can be a part of that progress." Pandini winked at the detectives and flashed his signature grin.

Plazinski finally spoke. "Mr. Pandini, I assure you that we will get this situation here at PPS under control. I hope you will be patient, and understanding. We've had some personnel changes, and this has resulted in—"

"I understand, of course," said Pandini smoothly. "I'm sure you'll have things under control in no time, Sergeant Plazinski. You always do."

Zengo couldn't believe what he had just heard. Was the sergeant going to let Pandini talk this way to members of his squad? Whose side was Plazinski on, anyway? Were some of Pandini's contributions going into Plazinski's pockets?

Zengo couldn't contain himself. "You're lying!" he shouted at Pandini. "I'm going to prove it!"

Pandini narrowed his eyes. Plazinski's bill hung

open. The two of them exchanged a glance. "I'll take care of this, Mr. Pandini," said Plazinski.

Pandini grinned at the sergeant. "I know I can count on you, Plazinski. I'm a manager, just like you. We can't let up a minute when it comes to supervising unruly staff members." He nodded at them all, rose from his seat, and left the office.

Plazinski stood silently at his window and watched Pandini's chauffeur place the tycoon securely in his car. Then he turned and ripped into his detectives.

"What in the what were you thinking? I told you

to stay away from Pandini! And now you're making headlines, shooting up his nightclub and arresting his busboy for no reason whatsoever!" Plazinski picked up his phone and threw it against the wall, ripping the cord out of the socket. Zengo winced at the sound of the mangled plastic crashing to the floor.

"But sir . . . we were just there to watch out for O'Malley's daughter. We weren't looking to arrest anyone, I promise!" He thought that might calm the sergeant down. But he was dead wrong.

Plazinski shifted his rage toward the senior detective. "O'Malley, your kid is old enough to go to a pep rally on her own. Don't you trust her?"

"Well, it's just that . . ."

"And don't you trust that I am giving you solid advice when I say to stay clear of Pandini? You should know better!"

Zengo raised his hand. "Sir, it was at my suggestion that we attended the pep rally, just to keep an eye on her."

"You were babysitting? Well I'll tell you what: I have no interest in babysitting my squad members! Now I'm going to be wasting my precious time getting you out of this hot water. This is a PR nightmare. It's going to be all over the papers tomorrow."

"But sir, listen," said Zengo desperately. "I may have been wrong about the busboy. But I swear I saw Hopkins at the club. He was there, at the pep rally. That's why I was in the back alley behind the club. I followed him there."

"Is that true, O'Malley?" said Plazinski. "Did you see the teacher too?"

O'Malley looked at Zengo. Then he looked at Plazinski. Then he looked back at Zengo. "I . . . I didn't actually see Hopkins myself, sir, no."

"There was no Hopkins, was there?" growled Plazinski, turning back to his rookie detective. "Just like there was NO BAG FULL OF ILLEGAL FISH. I've heard enough out of you two, especially you, Zengo. I expected more from you." He ran his hands through the fur on his head. "I have no choice: you're both off the case."

"B-b-but sir—!" O'Malley scrambled for the right words.

"B-b-but nothing! You two are an embarrassment to the badges you wear. And you're lucky I don't command you to turn them over this instant. Diaz and

172

Lucinni will be taking over, effective immediately. Starting tomorrow, the two of you are on crossing-guard duty. Report to the elementary school tomorrow morning. Now: get out of my office."

PLATYPUS POLICE SQUAD PARKING LOT, 10:45 P.M.

Zengo, furious and humiliated, stalked out to the parking lot. He could hear O'Malley hustling behind him. He didn't want to listen to what his partner had to say.

"I hope you're satisfied, rookie," said O'Malley. "You haven't heard a single thing I've said. You couldn't take the time to line up your evidence, didn't want to collect the facts and consider the next move. You just want to throw first and ask questions later. And what do you do tonight? You fly in all boomerangs a-blazing again. Now we're off the case. I need to go home and explain to my wife and kids that I've been demoted to crossing-guard duty. Never mind the fact that you've set this case back. If Hopkins is out there somewhere, the chances of anyone finding him are even slimmer now. What were you even thinking back there?"

Zengo just hung his head low.

"That's right—you weren't thinking!" O'Malley stood there with his flippers on his hips, doing a pretty good impersonation of Zengo's dad.

"I'm sorry," Zengo finally muttered, his head still hung low. He choked back tears. He couldn't believe he was almost crying in front of his partner. "I'm sorry. I didn't live up to expectations. I didn't do the right thing. I messed up."

"That's right. You did." O'Malley looked away and pursed his bill. "What is it with you and Pandini anyway? You're a smart kid. Why are you so bent on uncovering some conspiracy involving him?"

Zengo looked back up. He tried not to sniffle. "Pandini's father killed my grandpa."

O'Malley took a step back, shocked. "What do you mean?"

"My grandpa was in the PPS. Lieutenant Andrew Dailey. He led the team that took down Pandini, but he lost his life in the process. I just want to live up to his example, to make him proud. And I just have this feeling Pandini isn't what he seems. And no one seems to know it. I joined the force because I wanted to help people—and I thought that someone needed to keep an eye on him. I don't know . . . maybe I'm wrong."

"Lieutenant Dailey was your grandfather? He was my hero." Zengo could see O'Malley was in shock. "He was the bravest cop I ever knew."

Zengo shrugged. "That's why I didn't say anything. I guess I wanted to make it on my own. Maybe Pandini and I have something in common: we're both anxious not to be compared to the rest of our family." He took a deep breath, let it out. "Anyway, I'm sorry about tonight, about losing the case . . . about everything, O'Malley. I don't know what else to say."

O'Malley considered him for a moment. Then he took a deep breath too. "Look, rookie, get in the car. I'll drive you home."

"Nah, I think I'll just walk." Zengo gave a half wave good-bye and turned to leave. The rookie trudged sadly down the street, falling in and out of the dimly lit glow of the streetlamps. He heard O'Malley start up the car and drive away in the darkness.

GATES LANE ELEMENTARY SCHOOL, 8:45 A.M.

The line of cars easily stretched a mile down the road, out the parking lot of Gates Lane Elementary School and all the way down to the Palm Gardens shopping plaza. Crossing-guard duty should be a breeze, Zengo thought to himself as he directed traffic. But as another angry parent shook her fist at him, he couldn't help but think that getting another dressing-down from Plazinski might be easier.

Still, here he was, stuck wearing an orange sash and stopping cars so kids could kiss their parents good-bye before jumping out of the family minivans.

179

Even the kids at the elementary school were decked head-to-toe in Kal East football swag. The whole place was buzzing about the big game that evening, which just made Zengo's dismissal from the case sting even worse.

Zengo was lost in his thoughts when his tail was stomped upon by a butterball of a first grader. "Yee-ouch!" he yelled. The kid just stood there and stared at Zengo as he turned to rub his tail.

"Go on, get going," Zengo grumbled as he shooed the kid away. The first grader stuck his tongue out and then raced toward the school.

From the look of it, O'Malley wasn't enjoying his day any better. Zengo watched the pudgy kid run past his partner, who was stopping traffic by the drop-off area at the front entrance. Zengo looked miserably at him, embarrassed for both of them.

"C'mon, c'mon! Keep it moving!" Zengo yelled to the line of cars. He couldn't get the last student into the building quickly enough.

Fifteen minutes later, Zengo and O'Malley were sitting in their squad car. Neither had spoken much to the other, aside from a brief greeting this morning. O'Malley thumbed through a folder he'd brought. He flipped page after page, using the car's dashboard to organize the papers into piles.

Zengo tried his best to ignore O'Malley's busywork. He didn't even want to think about any other cases; it was too painful. But when the piles began falling into his lap, Zengo broke. "Dude! What is all of this?"

O'Malley looked up from the papers. "Phone messages. The ones Peggy has been passing along to Diaz and Lucinni."

"What are you doing with them?"

"I'm getting us out of this mess. But more importantly, I'm getting us closer to solving our case."

"It's not our case anymore, O'Malley, remember?"

O'Malley put the papers down. "Do you really

think Diaz and Lucinni are capable of getting to the bottom of this?"

Zengo looked out the passenger-side window. "O'Malley, I really thought I saw illegal fish in that kangaroo's bag. And I swear that was Hopkins in the club."

O'Malley placed his flipper on the paperwork. "I believe you. And that's why I brought these messages with me this morning. The sarge would have my hide if he knew we were still sniffing around the illegal fish epidemic, but I think that these messages are the key to getting to the bottom of the Hopkins case."

"*We?*"

"What? I assume you're still up for solving this case, rookie."

Zengo smiled for the first time that day. "You know it, partner." Zengo was impressed by O'Malley's gumption. Plazinski would surely fire him altogether if he got word of this. Zengo thought of the family his partner needed to support—finding Hopkins just became all the more crucial.

"Well, then listen up: I've been going through the fine print on these switchboard messages, and it looks like most of the calls from the past few days have come from the same number. A pay phone down-town. Not far from Bamboo."

Zengo's eyes widened. "You think there's someone in Pandini's crew who has been trying to get in touch with the PPS?"

"I'm not sure what to make of this. But I bet there's a connection."

"Look, O'Malley," Zengo started. "I know I can't make up for what I've done already. But closing this case means everything to me. I won't let you down."

"I know it, rookie." O'Malley looked at his partner. "And I'm glad you told me that Lieutenant Dailey was your grandfather. He was one of the most driven cops I've ever known. There aren't many detectives who have the fire that he did. But I think I might have been paired up with one."

Zengo didn't have a chance to respond before the recess bell rang. The school yard was flooded with young kids tripping over their untied shoelaces.

O'Malley looked back at Zengo. "Duty calls. We take care of these munchkins, and then we investigate this pay phone. What do you say?"

"Game on!" Zengo shook O'Malley's flipper and tightened his crossing-guard sash.

SOUTHSIDE KALAMAZOO, 3:00 P.M.

Zengo and O'Malley peeled out of the elementary
school parking lot the minute the last kindergartners
were safely inside their parents' cars. They barreled
down the suburban streets, and once they were on the
highway, O'Malley put the pedal to the floor, speed-
ing past a series of billboards advertising the Kal
East Pandas' first game at the new stadium. Soon the
downtown skyscrapers rose up before them, and the
detectives were turning off the highway and navigat-
ing the southside city streets. Zengo held one of the
phone messages in his hand as they passed Bamboo
on their left.

"There!" he said, pointing to a pay phone on the corner of Broad Street and Fifth. O'Malley pulled over, and the partners stepped out of the car, leaving their orange sashes behind.

They inspected the pay phone but couldn't find anything out of the ordinary. Zengo couldn't help but feel disappointed. He didn't exactly expect the caller to be right there, waiting to be discovered, but he was hoping to at least find a clue of some sort.

"Another dead end."

"Not so fast, rookie," said O'Malley. "You don't see anything odd about this phone?"

"You mean aside from the fact that it's a pay phone?" Not many people used them these days. Zengo didn't know anyone who didn't have a cell, and this phone looked more like an antique than anything else.

"That's *exactly* what I mean. It's not a cell phone, and it's not a house line. Whoever the caller was—and I think we can assume that it wasn't multiple people making the same calls to the station about illegal fish from this particular pay phone—they must have not had access to another phone, or they were looking to hide their identity."

Zengo scanned the area, and grabbed O'Malley's elbow. "Look!"

He pointed down Broad Street. About a block and a half down stood an impressive building with fluted columns and a domed roof—the Kalamazoo Public Library. "Are you thinking what I'm thinking?"

"Let's check it out," said O'Malley.

They jogged down the street to the library entrance, alert, like bloodhounds on a fresh scent.

The detectives entered the front foyer of the library. The ceilings stretched up what seemed like miles. The art on the walls was all original, and the hardwood floors creaked with each step. Zengo looked around, not sure where to go. He hadn't been in a library for some time. O'Malley made for an information desk in the center of the sprawling space. He led Zengo past computers, magazine racks, and shelves upon shelves of books. As they strolled up to the desk, they took off their sunglasses in unison. Behind the desk, a librarian looked up from her paperwork.

"Hello, ma'am," Zengo said, he and O'Malley flashing their badges. "We're from the Platypus Police Squad."

She seemed startled by the badges. Zengo figured

it probably wasn't every day that cops came snooping around her library. But she had a funny look on her face as she checked Zengo out. He felt a little uncomfortable. "Is there . . . something wrong, Officer?"

"It's Detective, ma'am," said O'Malley. The librarian didn't take her eyes off Zengo. "And no, not that we know of. We're just wondering if anyone might have been spending a lot of time here over the past week or so."

She didn't answer.

"Ma'am?" asked Zengo.

Finally she seemed to snap out of it. "What? Well,

there is this one guy," she said. "I think he might be homeless. He has been coming in all week, leaving periodically for a minute or two and returning, usually to the legal section."

"Thanks very much, ma'am," said Zengo.

"Oh, anytime. And if you, you know, need any books . . ." She laughed nervously. "Well, you know where I am!"

"Got it," said O'Malley, turning Zengo away. "Thanks again."

The detectives took a few steps. Then Zengo stopped. He looked at O'Malley, who just shrugged. The both spun around. "Er, ma'am—"

The librarian was still looking at Zengo. "Upstairs, take a right, and then all the way at the end of the row on the left."

"Thanks."

They turned to leave once again. They looked left. They looked right. They still hadn't taken a step forward when the librarian said, "The stairs are behind the circulation desk and to the right, or if you would prefer to take the elevator, it's next to the restrooms, which are just down this way past periodicals and to the left."

The detectives put on their sunglasses and jogged up the stairs. They passed college students hunched over research papers, librarians pushing book carts, and mountains of books. At last they came upon the legal section.

At first glance, it appeared that no one had been in the section for a while. But then, Zengo elbowed O'Malley and nodded toward a grouping of comfortable chairs by a bay of windows. A lone figure sat in one of the chairs. Books were stacked up on the table beside the chair, as well as a ratty old backpack. Beside that lay a vintage black-and-red Kal East Pirates baseball cap.

Zengo whispered, "O'Malley! The hat!" Zengo stepped toward the chairs, but O'Malley pulled him back behind a bookshelf.

"We wait," O'Malley whispered. They pulled out a few books and peered through the shelves. A few minutes went by, and the man stood up, placed the cap upon his head, placed the books in his backpack, and turned to leave. As if on cue, Zengo and O'Malley darted from either side of the bookshelf, surrounding the stunned figure.

"Professor Hopkins," O'Malley said as he flashed

his badge. "We got your messages."

The professor, after a moment of shock, seemed to process what they had said, and exhaled. "Finally," he said.

PLATYPUS POLICE SQUAD HEADQUARTERS, 3:45 P.M.

Zengo and O'Malley marched into the station with a weathered-looking Professor Hopkins in tow. They passed Diaz and Lucinni, who were sitting at their desks with their feet up. They were tossing a football back and forth, but at the sight of the frog, they jerked upright in their seats, sending the football thumping to the ground. Zengo and O'Malley made a beeline across the floor, not even giving Diaz and Lucinni a second look, straight for Plazinski's office in the back. But before they could reach the sergeant's office door, it swung open.

Zengo realized that furious was the new normal, as far as Plazinski was concerned.

"Where have you two been?" shouted the sergeant. "Crossing-guard duty ended an hour and a half ago! You were to return to the station immediately and—"

O'Malley cut him off. "We were solving a missing-person case." He and Zengo pulled Hopkins forward. Plazinski's fists relaxed, and his enraged expression gave way to awed bewilderment.

"*And* an illegal fish case," said Zengo.

Diaz and Lucinni stumbled over themselves as they reached the unfolding scene. "Sarge, this was our case!"

"You're right. It *was* your case. Everybody in the interrogation room. NOW!"

A few minutes later, Hopkins nursed a cup of coffee while the sergeant sat across from him. O'Malley and Zengo stood by the windowless wall. Diaz and Lucinni squared off on the opposite side of the room by the one-way mirror. The pairs locked eyes like tag-team wrestlers about to battle for the title. Hopkins sipped his coffee and told his story, every word helping to unravel the tangled web the Platypus Police Squad had been grappling with.

"I couldn't help but notice all the fish in school, and I knew that some of it, if not all of it, must have been illegal. I remember years back, when Frank Pandini Sr. was around, and illegal fish almost destroyed the school and the city, driving a wedge between the rich and the poor. It hadn't been a problem for over a decade, and things had gotten so much better. But if it was in the schools, well, a lot of good people were going to lose their jobs, including the parents of some of my favorite students. And when kids started missing classes because they got ahold of some bad fish, I couldn't take things sitting down. I tried calling the PPS, to let you know something was happening. In

fact, I made many calls, but every message went unanswered." Plazinski turned in his seat and shot Diaz and Lucinni a look that could pierce steel. The detectives shifted their weight and averted their gazes.

Zengo mouthed, "High five," and he and O'Malley quietly slapped flippers. Their arms were crossed again by the time Plazinski turned back to Hopkins.

"I apologize for that oversight. I will be launching a full internal investigation. Please, continue."

"Well, with more and more illegal fish flooding the hallways and the spotlight about to be cast on Kal East with the big football game coming up, I decided someone needed to get to the bottom of who was the source at the high school. And while I couldn't figure out who in the school was selling illegal fish, I was able to follow the trail to the supplier: a boxer named Joey."

Plazinski glanced at Zengo. It took every ounce of the rookie's willpower not to say anything. He just stood there with his arms crossed.

"And how exactly did you discover all of this?" asked Plazinski as he turned a page in his notebook.

"Fortunately, one of my students was as concerned about illegal fish in the school as I was. It was the information he gave me that led me to Joey."

"And what student was this?" asked Plazinski as he scribbled down notes.

Hopkins looked down at his coffee. "I can't tell you. I don't want him in any more danger than I've already put him in."

"It's Shawn Freeman, isn't it, sir?" asked O'Malley.

"Shawn? No," said Hopkins, surprised. "It's true, his father was one of the fishermen whose job was threatened by the illegal fish trade, but he wasn't the student who was helping me."

"Who was it then?" asked Zengo. "I assure you, the information will be kept confidential."

Hopkins let out a deep sigh. He looked to both pairs of detectives and to Plazinski. "Blake Cameron. He works out at the same gym as Joey and did some snooping around, often opting to walk home after his team's weight sessions. I planned an illegal fish trade of my own so that I could be sure it was Joey. Blake didn't want me to—said it was too dangerous. I swore him to secrecy. As you can imagine, out of context, a high school teacher involved with an illegal fish trade would not exactly reflect well on my character."

The information hit Zengo like a ton of fish. Blake's

skittishness around them suddenly made sense. He didn't have a guilty conscience; he wasn't scared of his girlfriend's dad—he wanted to keep his word and protect his teacher.

"And so you set up a deal. What happened?" Plazinski was still taking notes as quickly as he could.

"Well, Blake and I were hoping that Joey might reveal the name of the student or teacher who was piping the illegal fish into the high school. Blake set up a time and place with Joey on my behalf. We were to meet at the docks after nightfall. Everything was going as planned. Joey turned up and sold me a big duffel bag filled with illegal fish. I had the evidence I needed. I was going to immediately come here, to you guys, to report everything I had learned.

"But someone must have gotten wise to what I was up to. This somebody tried to run me down, right there on the docks. It was no accident; they came gunning for me, their car barreling down the pier. Fortunately, I was able to jump in the water right before the car struck. I swam to safety and have been lying low ever since."

"Did you see who was driving the car?"

"It all happened so quickly. But for a split second,

before I leaped to safety, I caught a glimpse of the driver."

Everyone leaned forward. "And . . . ," Plazinski said.

"Well, I can't be sure, but I am fairly certain . . . it was Frank Pandini Jr."

Plazinksi fell back in his chair. Diaz and Lucinni looked at each other in disbelief. Zengo saw O'Malley glance over at him, but he could barely move or think. *It was Pandini?*

"I thought it would be too dangerous to come into PPS headquarters without first speaking with someone, making myself known. So I called from a pay phone near the library a few times a day. Gave the receptionist the number of the pay phone, hoping I might get a call back. But I never did." Everybody shot daggers at Diaz and Lucinni, who seemed to be trying as hard as they could to sink into the floor.

"Anyway, I know when the next illegal fish deal is going down: tonight, at the big game. Joey's been making most of his deals at big school events. With so many people attending the opening of the new stadium, no one will notice a deal happening—and he'll have no shortage of customers."

Plazinski shut his notebook. "Professor, thank you.

You have gone above and beyond your duty as a citizen. The Platypus Police Squad will handle it from here. We're going to get you into protective custody for the time being. And we'll be at the game tonight to get to the bottom of this. Zengo, O'Malley—you're officially back on the case. Diaz, Lucinni—you'll be providing backup. Whatever Detective O'Malley and Detective Zengo need, you will do as they instruct."

Zengo liked the sound of that. The rookie puffed up his chest. They were back on the case! He turned to O'Malley, about to give him a big hug, but thought better of it. O'Malley seemed to be thinking the same thing. Diaz and Lucinni didn't look happy, but under the circumstances, they were probably relieved they wouldn't be ending up on crossing-guard duty.

Plazinski stood up. "What are we waiting for? Let's do this."

EAST KALAMAZOO MIDDLE SCHOOL/HIGH SCHOOL FOOTBALL STADIUM, 7:45 P.M.

Kal East was alive with excitement. The seats were packed, folks from all over the city in attendance for the biggest game in the history of the school. The new stadium glistened under the state-of-the-art floodlights. The huge Pandatron hung above the scoreboard, bringing real-time video from all the other games in the state, interspersed with noisy commercials for every one of the Pandini projects.

Students who had never experienced a night game on home turf buzzed with the excitement and hope of a victory. They were facing last year's champs, and whichever team was undefeated today would just about guarantee them a pathway to compete for this year's state championship. The die-hards were painted head to toe in the school colors, red and black. The parents' booster club was selling commemorative T-shirts by the entrance. Everyone in town was there—rich, poor, young, old, even people who didn't like sports but who were proud of their town and their team.

The cheerleaders looked fantastic in their new uniforms. Vanessa led them in a rousing rendition of the new P-A-N-D-A-S cheer. She smiled toward the sidelines, where Blake was getting ready to take the field. Shawn Freeman did a series of backflips—he'd clearly gotten used to the new mascot costume.

And in the VIP section, right at the fifty-yard line, sat Pandini himself. He was decked out in an extra-large Kal East sweatshirt and a Kal East cap. Next to him were Principal McKeever and Mayor Saunders.

Monte Belmonte, the announcer and star DJ at Z94.3, was pumping up the crowd. He played Roxie's latest hit, and the crowd roared. The bleachers were a sea of waving red-and-black pennants.

Amid all the excitement, the fans didn't even notice another group decked out in school colors: the Platypus Police Squad. Detectives Rick Zengo, Corey O'Malley, Carlos Diaz, and Eddie Lucinni blended in with the crowd, wearing Kal East caps low on their brows. Zengo watched as the other detectives took up their positions at the conces-sion stand (O'Malley had already gotten himself a hot dog, and Zengo's stomach grumbled), the main entrance to the field, and the northeast corner of the field. Zengo, positioned right beside the home bleachers, continued to scan the crowd. He flicked on his radio.

"Any movement, O'Malley?"

"Nothing here, partner. Diaz? Lucinni?"

"We got nothing, boys."

Zengo dropped his flipper, frustrated. This was it, their best chance at cracking this case. As the Pandas took the field for the opening kickoff, he surveyed the bleachers again. And that was when he saw it.

One of the thousands of Kal East caps in the stands wasn't looking at the ball the kicker had just placed on the tee.

It was moving toward the stairs.

To be precise, it was *bouncing* toward the stairs.

Zengo brought his radio back up to his bill. "This is Zengo. I've got eyes on Joey. Repeat: he's in my sights. Everyone converge on the west side of the bleachers."

All three detectives were soon by Zengo's side. They huddled behind the medic truck that was parked nearby, their location giving them a clear view of Joey, who had taken up a position under the bleachers and stood alone, waiting. A stuffed Roar duffel bag was slung across his shoulder, and while he shifted his gaze from side to side, he seemed unaware of the four detectives keeping watch.

"He's alone," Diaz said. "This is our chance to take him." But Zengo pulled him back.

"No. We wait. We need to know what's in that duffel before we go rushing in." Zengo placed binoculars up to his eyes and focused in on Joey's bag. When he dropped the glasses for a moment and looked around, he saw O'Malley smiling at him. Maybe he was beginning to get the hang of this thing after all.

Another minute went by. Joey was clearly getting antsy. He looked over his shoulder and zipped open his duffel. There, in plain view, where all the detectives could see it—illegal fish.

"Move," O'Malley commanded, and the four web-footed detectives charged the bleachers. Diaz and Lucinni moved around to cover the central aisle in case Joey tried to escape that way, while Zengo and O'Malley moved on him from the far side.

As they rounded the corner, Joey looked up and

spotted them. He dropped the bag and bolted.

"He's on the move!" O'Malley drew his boomerang and made a perfect throw at Joey's legs. He stumbled for a moment, but that was long enough. Zengo sailed through the air and was on top of him, both of them slamming into the ground. Joey struggled, but it was no use. Zengo had his arms pulled behind him tightly. Diaz tore around the corner and tossed Zengo a set of handcuffs, which he locked in place. Lucinni, a boomerang trained on Joey, started reading him his rights.

Zengo rolled away and lay on his back for a moment. There was a flipper in his view. O'Malley's. He helped Zengo to his feet.

"Nice shot, old-timer," said Zengo.

"Nice tackle, rookie."

They smiled at each other. But that was when Zengo realized they weren't alone. Another figure had come around the edge of the bleachers. The person Joey must have been waiting for.

"Joey, if this is going to happen, it's got to happen now—"

Zengo and O'Malley looked toward the end of the bleachers.

Frank Pandini Jr. turned the corner. The detectives stood in shocked silence. But only for a moment.

"Freeze!" said Zengo. "Don't move, Pandini!" He and O'Malley both drew their boomerangs.

Pandini turned and ran. Zengo took off after him, hearing O'Malley behind him give an order to Diaz and Lucinni to stay with Joey.

Pandini was about fifteen yards ahead of Zengo when he hit the crowds in front of the bleachers, pushing students and parents out of his way. Zengo darted through the crowd, O'Malley not far behind him. Pandini, never looking back, grabbed a trash can and threw it right into Zengo's path. He cleared it with a leap, but Pandini had already opened up some distance as he reached the sideline. *Man, Pandini is fast for a big guy*, Zengo thought. Zengo threw it into high gear and gained on him, as O'Malley fell behind.

By now, the crowd had clearly spotted them. Pandini was finally slowing down, almost close enough for Zengo to leap and grab him. That was when he made a left turn—right onto the field.

"The Pandas are set up for a third and two," announced Monte Belmonte. "And . . . ladies and gentlemen, something is happening down in the Pandas' end zone. . . . It appears that Frank Pandini has taken the field!" The crowd went wild; everyone got to their feet and applauded. "I'm not sure what's going on, but the refs have waived the play dead. . . ."

Zengo tuned out the announcer and tore onto the field after Pandini; he didn't even notice that this entire kerfuffle was being broadcast on the Pandatron screen. O'Malley was nowhere in sight, and Zengo hoped the old guy wasn't passed out somewhere. Vanessa and the rest of the cheerleaders scattered, and the athletes dropped to the ground when they saw Zengo's boomerang. With the field finally open, Pandini ran for the main exit. Zengo was trying to find one more push to catch him before he escaped when he saw his partner appear at the other end of the field, right in Pandini's path. O'Malley withdrew his boomerang, reeled back, and threw it, another perfect shot taking out Pandini's legs. "Get him, Zengo!" O'Malley shouted.

Pandini was back on his feet and, while limping, making a break for the crowd. Zengo leaped and tackled him to the ground, his massive form slamming into the turf. The crowd gasped, cameras flashed, and Zengo was practically dead with exhaustion. He pulled himself up, got a set of cuffs from off his belt, and slapped them onto Pandini's wrists.

"You have the right to remain silent," Zengo began as O'Malley ran up by his side. The two of them shared a look. But then they were both engulfed in a huge shadow. They turned and found themselves staring up at . . .

Frank Pandini Jr.?

"Gentlemen, what exactly is going on?" the tycoon asked. He was flanked by the mayor, the principal, and a gaggle of press, including Derek Doherty, who snapped away with his camera.

Zengo and O'Malley looked at each other and then down at the person they had just arrested. Now that he wasn't moving, Zengo got a better look at him. There was a zipper running up the back of the Kal East sweatshirt.

It wasn't Pandini at all. It was the Kal East Pandas' mascot. Zengo and O'Malley pulled off the head to reveal the dirty, frightened face of Shawn Freeman.

"I can explain," Shawn started.

Zengo and O'Malley looked up as a giant flashbulb went off in their faces.

"Gold! Pure gold!" said Derek Doherty as he snapped another photo.

EAST KALAMAZOO MIDDLE/HIGH SCHOOL OFFICE, 9:00 P.M.

After the excitement died down, the detectives helped the referees clear the field so the game could continue. Diaz and Lucinni took Joey back to the station for processing while Zengo and O'Malley led Shawn to Principal McKeever's office. Plazinski met them there. And Shawn related his story.

"I'm the one responsible for selling illegal fish in the school. Illegal fish were all over town, putting genuine fishermen out of business, and my dad was going to lose his job. My family needed the money, and this seemed like the easiest way to get it. I'd been trying to convince my dad for years to consider selling synthetic fish, but he would never listen to me. I thought that maybe this would be my chance to prove to him I was right. I met Joey at Bamboo a while back, and he made me a deal. With every sale I arranged, he gave me a ten-percent commission."

"Shawn, I can't believe this," said Principal McKeever. Zengo and O'Malley shared a look while Plazinski crossed his arms, but said nothing. Shawn swallowed and continued.

"It seemed so easy at first, and the sales were so small that no one suspected anything. But then it started getting out of hand. The past couple weeks we did five times the business we did just a month ago. And Professor Hopkins started to figure things out. I couldn't bear the thought of him discovering what I was up to. He was my favorite teacher. I had no choice. I had to scare him off. I never would have hit him with my car! I knew he'd jump in the water. He's a frog. That's what they do. I didn't think that he'd just disappear, and call attention to what was going on."

"Why did you try to frame Blake?" O'Malley asked.

"I knew Blake was getting together with Hopkins

after school, way more than if he were just getting extra help. I realized he was probably helping Hopkins with his investigation. So I figured that if I pointed you guys in his direction, you'd find their after-school meetings suspicious. . . ." Shawn trailed off and hung his head.

Zengo could see how sorry he was. He didn't seem like a bad kid. More like a desperate kid who made a bunch of mistakes and got in too deep. But he got involved in the illegal fish trade and could have seriously injured his teacher. *It doesn't matter how hard things have been for his family; there's no excuse.*

There was a knock at the door. "Come in," Plazinski called out. Peter, the fisherman they had met the other day, entered.

"I got a call from the PPS, tellin' me they ah questionin' my son. . . . What's happenin'?"

"Mr. Freeman, I'm sorry to have to tell you this—," Plazinski started, but Zengo interrupted him.

"Shawn needs to tell you something. The rest of us can wait outside."

O'Malley gave the slightest nod to Zengo. Plazinski didn't move for a moment, then he, too, nodded and led his detectives back into the waiting room outside the office while Shawn started talking to his dad.

"The kid's going to have to stand up in juvenile court for his part in this, but his testimony should help us get Joey behind bars," said the sarge after he had closed the door. "Boy, this is one of the wildest cases I've seen since we put Frank Pandini Sr. away. Now don't get me wrong. Zengo, you're a loose cannon, and I think you need a lesson or two in how the game is played. And O'Malley, I'm going to be honest, you need to lose a few pounds. But darn it, that was some of the best detective work I've seen out of this unit in years. You should both be proud of yourselves."

Zengo's heart practically leaped out of his chest. He turned to O'Malley, who had a smile on his bill— or, at least, what passed for a smile on O'Malley.

"Zengo, I want you to listen to O'Malley from here on out, and listen good. He knows his stuff. O'Malley, I have to say, it's good to see a little bit of spring in your

218

step again. It's been too long."

"Zengo and O'Malley REPRESENT!" said Zengo. O'Malley stared at him for a moment, but then high-fived Zengo's waiting flipper.

"All right, all right," he said. "I don't want to be *those* guys, but I also can't leave my partner hanging." Even the sarge smirked at that.

But before any of them could say another word, the door to the waiting room opened.

It was Frank Pandini Jr.

"Detectives, Sergeant," Pandini said. "I just wanted you to know how very embarrassing this is for Pandini Enterprises. I am absolutely shocked that Joey was running his illegal fish trade out of Bamboo, right under my nose. I will be conducting a full investigation of all of my businesses, you can count on this. And I will, of course, be providing full cooperation to the Platypus Police Squad in any way I can. The illegal fish trade brought my father down and brought shame on my family, and I do hope that anyone found to be dealing in illegal fish will be treated accordingly. I can promise you that such will be so in the Pandini empire. This behavior will not stand. Not in my businesses, not in our city."

Zengo narrowed his eyes, but he bit his bill, forcing himself to remain silent. Maybe he was learning the ropes after all. In any case, he was glad to not feel O'Malley's heel grinding into his foot.

"Thank you very much, Mr. Pandini," said Plazinski. "I'm sure we'll have some more questions for you in the coming days. Our office will arrange an appointment with your secretary, if that meets with your approval."

"Yes, of course." Pandini proceeded back through the door, but turned before closing it. "Oh, and gentlemen, please—do accept my invitation to attend this evening's postgame celebration at Bamboo. Root beer floats are on the house for Kalamazoo's finest." He flashed his signature grin before his massive figure disappeared down the hallway.

Through the windows the detectives heard the stadium erupt in applause as Monte Belmonte announced another Kal East touchdown. They got back to the field in time to see Blake throw one more, just as time expired. A Kal East victory was already a done deal, but it was still a sweet play for the boys in red. *Gravy*, thought Zengo. The Kal East fans rushed the field, and Blake was hoisted into the air. Zengo saw Blake, beaming, looking across the field to catch Vanessa's eye. She blew him a kiss. O'Malley suddenly became very interested in something on the ground at his feet.

"Hey, old-timer, look on the bright side," said Zengo. "At least now we know he's not an illegal fish dealer and a killer."

"I suppose that is *a* bright side," humphed O'Malley.

BAMBOO, 10:45 P.M.

That night at Bamboo, O'Malley and Zengo clinked root beer mugs, complete with red-and-black mini umbrellas. They were surrounded by revelers decked out in school colors.

"You know," said Zengo, barely audible above Roxie's singing, "I still don't trust Pandini, but I'm not going to turn down a free float."

"Keep your friends close and your enemies closer," said O'Malley as he took a swig. He wiped the ice cream mustache off his bill. "And trust or not, his hot dogs are out of this world. Taste much better than ketchup packets, son."

Vanessa sneaked up behind her dad and kissed him on the cheek. "You were so brave back there, Daddy!"

O'Malley was clearly caught off guard. "It's what I do, cupcake."

"Do you think I'll be able to stay out an hour past curfew?" She raised her eyebrows and flashed a smile. "Pleeeeease?"

O'Malley gave his partner a look. "There's certainly an art to getting what you want," said Zengo, offering his partner a smile and a shrug of the shoulders.

"I'll give you thirty minutes past curfew, not a minute more," said O'Malley, turning back to his daughter. "Now get back to your friends. You're cramping my style!"

"Thanks, Daddy!"

Blake came over and took Vanessa by the hand and spun her around. He looked to O'Malley, who nodded to him. Blake nodded back. He and Vanessa returned to the dance floor to shake their tails. Vanessa's girlfriends all whispered to one another and kept looking at Zengo. O'Malley cocked an eyebrow at him and he rolled his eyes, holding his glass out for a clink. They both took a giant gulp and smiled.

Up in Bamboo's second-floor office, Frank Pandini Jr. stood watching the revelry on the dance floor below. He was once again dressed in his trademark white tuxedo, affixing his newest pair of diamond cuff links. He was not smiling.

"Bobby, come here, please."

The security guard lumbered across the office to the one-way tinted glass wall and looked where Pandini was looking.

"I want you to move our inventory. With Joey in custody, we can't take any risks. He won't squeal, or finger any of our other dealers, but he may be talked into revealing one of our fish-processing locations. He's never been the smart one in his family."

Bobby smirked.

"And find out what happened with our last supply. Why it went bad. We can't allow a disaster like this to happen again." He finished adjusting his cuff links and rubbed his temples. "I can't believe my business was nearly sunk because of a case of bad fish and a nosy schoolteacher. This will not happen again. Do you understand me, Bobby?"

His security guard nodded. "Sir . . . what about the two detectives?"

Pandini looked down at Zengo and O'Malley. He narrowed his eyes. "I want you to keep a close eye on them. That Detective Zengo is Lieutenant Dailey's grandson, and I can tell he's not going to give us any breathing room. As for O'Malley . . ." Pandini glanced up at Bobby for the first time. "Well, you remember what Dad said about him."

Bobby shifted uncomfortably.

"Yes, Bobby. Let's make sure they keep coming in here." He cracked his knuckles and finally turned back to his desk. "Keep your friends close, and your enemies closer."

ACKNOWLEDGMENTS

A thank-you to Jordan Brown, without whom I wouldn't have graduated the academy. I wear my middle-grade chapter-book badge because of your diligence. I am grateful for the unflagging support and dedication from Rebecca Sherman, who has hit the beat with me time and time again. For the indelible support from Deb Shapiro, who is masterfully handling dispatch. For Eddie Gamarra, who told me "penguins are done in this town." It is these absurd but very real conversations that make it all happen.

For Kellie and Deb at Walden to Casey and Tom at HarperCollins, it is an honor to partner with such a remarkable and talented team! And for the Platypus Police Squad West Coast operations: Dick, Tony, Deb, Alex, and Jim.

Thank you to my real-world cop friends Corey McGrath and Chris Zengo, as well as Officer Sean Casella and everyone at the Northampton Police Department. Thank you for answering all of my questions. For the 1998 Yellow Platypus at the Hole in the Wall Gang Camp, my first instance of drawing a monotreme.

Thank you to Joey Weiser and Michele Chidester for their help in shading the art in this book. You are the patron saints of deadlines.

And most importantly, thank you to my girls—Gina, Zoe, and Lucy—for their constant and unparalleled support and patience. And yes, for Ralph, too. You do a remarkable job of taking pug naps in the studio.

JARRETT J. KROSOCZKA

is the author and illustrator of the Lunch Lady graphic novel series, a two-time winner of the Children's Choice Book Award, as well as many picture books. He can be heard on "The Book Report with JJK," his radio segment on SiriusXM's Kids Place Live. Jarrett lives in Northampton, Massachusetts, with his wife, two daughters, and their pug, Ralph Macchio. You can visit him online at www.studiojjk.com.

For exclusive information on your favorite authors
and artists, visit www.authortracker.com.

Also available as an ebook.

Zengo and O'Malley will return in . . .

PLATYPUS POLICE SQUAD:
THE OSTRICH CONSPIRACY

The opening of the Kalamazoo City Dome—the world's largest indoor amusement complex—has everyone in the city buzzing, especially because it's going to be the shooting site for Chase Mercy's new blockbuster film. But that's when things start to go haywire. Who could want to sabotage the Dome, and why? KC's finest are on the case!